Behind Closed Doors

Also From Skye Warren

Rochester Series
Private Property
Strict Confidence
Best Kept Secret
Hiding Places

North Security Trilogy & more North brothers
Overture
Concerto
Sonata
Audition
Diamond in the Rough
Silver Lining
Gold Mine
Finale

Endgame Trilogy & more books in Tanglewood
The Pawn
The Knight
The Castle
The King
The Queen
Escort
Survival of the Richest
The Evolution of Man
Mating Theory
The Bishop

For a complete listing of Skye Warren books, visit
www.skyewarren.com/books

Behind Closed Doors

A Rochester Novella

By Skye Warren

1001 DARK NIGHTS
PRESS

Behind Closed Doors
A Rochester Novella
By Skye Warren

1001 Dark Nights
Copyright 2022 Skye Warren
ISBN: 978-1-951812-96-6

Foreword: Copyright 2014 M. J. Rose

Published by 1001 Dark Nights Press, an imprint of Evil Eye Concepts, Incorporated

Acknowledgments from the Author

Thank you so much to Liz, Jillian, and MJ for allowing me to be part of the 1,001 Dark Nights family. I'm grateful to be here.

One Thousand and One Dark Nights

Once upon a time, in the future…

I was a student fascinated with stories and learning.
I studied philosophy, poetry, history, the occult, and
the art and science of love and magic. I had a vast
library at my father's home and collected thousands
of volumes of fantastic tales.

I learned all about ancient races and bygone
times. About myths and legends and dreams of all
people through the millennium. And the more I read
the stronger my imagination grew until I discovered
that I was able to travel into the stories... to actually
become part of them.

I wish I could say that I listened to my teacher
and respected my gift, as I ought to have. If I had, I
would not be telling you this tale now.
But I was foolhardy and confused, showing off
with bravery.

One afternoon, curious about the myth of the
Arabian Nights, I traveled back to ancient Persia to
see for myself if it was true that every day Shahryar
(Persian: شهريار, "king") married a new virgin, and then
sent yesterday's wife to be beheaded. It was written
and I had read that by the time he met Scheherazade,
the vizier's daughter, he'd killed one thousand
women.

*Something went wrong with my efforts. I arrived
in the midst of the story and somehow exchanged
places with Scheherazade — a phenomena that had
never occurred before and that still to this day, I
cannot explain.*

*Now I am trapped in that ancient past. I have
taken on Scheherazade's life and the only way I can
protect myself and stay alive is to do what she did to
protect herself and stay alive.*

*Every night the King calls for me and listens as I spin tales.
And when the evening ends and dawn breaks, I stop at a
point that leaves him breathless and yearning for more.
And so the King spares my life for one more day, so that
he might hear the rest of my dark tale.*

*As soon as I finish a story... I begin a new
one... like the one that you, dear reader, have before
you now.*

Chapter One

Marjorie

The scent of warm leather fills me with a deep-rooted peace.

I place the stitched vellum into place between the marbled endpapers. My heartbeat is slow, my breathing steady. Bookbinding is a meditative work. It's about ritual and care more than efficiency. It started as a way to fill the hours when the inn had no guests, a way to make money during Maine's off season. It's become so much more than that.

The last of my guests left two weeks ago. An adorable couple looking for shelter from the cold front. They live in a converted Airstream, going from city to city. National park to national park. They enjoy the nomadic lifestyle, but even they wanted central heating for a few nights.

Some inns close down during the winter months, but I don't see the point. This is my home. I'm here anyway, so I may as well leave the door unlocked for someone who needs a room.

Lighthouse Inn is not only my personal safe haven. It's a place where anyone can stop and rest for the night. I know how lonely life on the road can be. I offer them a warm bed and a smile before they continue on with their journey.

Shadows lurk in the corners of my mind. Memories from when I needed a safe place.

I couldn't find a haven then, but I made it for myself.

The bone folder. A cutting blade. Archival quality glue. My tools line up beside me, clean and sharp. This, too, is part of my ritual. I enjoy the ritual of it.

And mostly, the sense that I'm building something permanent.

The bell rings.

It's the bell over the front door, heralding the arrival of someone. A guest? No. There are no reservations on the books for weeks. And the weather has turned stormy. No one would be out at a time like this. I get deliveries, but not at this hour.

I put away the book and head into the lobby, already smiling in anticipation of greeting someone.

A man stands in the entryway, raindrops sliding down a black trench coat.

My smile fades.

The lobby is comfortably small, only big enough for guests to check in with their luggage in tow. It feels even smaller now with the dark, imposing figure looming. The air feels thick, as if he's filling it with his presence. Dark eyes and black hair. He holds a utilitarian black duffel bag that feels incongruous against the homey backdrop walls.

Dangerous.

It's the first word that springs to mind as I stare at him.

But also handsome.

I swallow around the knot in my throat. "Welcome to the Lighthouse Inn. Do you have a reservation?" I ask while I tap the keyboard to pull up the calendar. I know he doesn't have one. I ask anyway because it sets the tone between us.

I'm the owner of the inn.

He's a guest. Nothing more, nothing less.

"No reservation." The low gravel of his voice runs over my spine.

Hesitation holds me in its grip. I have to force the words out around the knot of tension in my throat. "Would you like a room? We have an opening."

He looks around, and I have the strange sense that he can see through the walls, that he knows we're completely empty. "Something overlooking the ocean."

"Absolutely. Most of our rooms have stunning views. Some with their own private balconies. There's a corner suite available if that's—"

"Any of them will work." He growls the words. Everything about him is rough, textured, hard. It makes me feel like a cat. I want to rub myself against him, the way a bear pushes against a tree. Because his edges would feel good against me.

"I've booked your room. Are you traveling for business or pleasure?"

He offers a small, humorless smile. "Business. There's no pleasure here."

A shiver runs through me. The desolation in his tone strikes a chord inside me. A chord of remembrance. Of empathy. I know what hopelessness feels like. It makes me determined that he enjoy his stay here. "How long would you like the room?"

He hesitates, his brown eyes darkening. "Three days."

There's something strange about the way he says them. As if they're a lie. Which is a strange thought to have. Why would he lie about that? I don't know, but my gut feels certain he's not telling me the whole truth. Well, that's all right.

Guests are allowed their secrets.

Just as the innkeeper is allowed hers.

I push the old-fashioned ledger across the scarred oak countertop, showing him where he can fill out his information and quoting him our off-season rates for the room.

He grips the pen with a casual strength. *Sam Smith,* he writes.

A fake name? I don't let my expression betray me. "Can I see your ID?"

He pulls out his wallet and sets down a stack of cash on the desk. Without counting, I'm guessing it's enough to cover all three nights. At least I know I'll get paid—even if he's bullshitting about his name.

But I should still demand to see identification.

It's a normal part of checking into inns and hotels. Only the seediest motels allow people to pay cash only with a fake name. He studies me, his waiting almost fatalistic, as if he's expecting me to turn him away.

It makes my heart clench.

I know what it's like to be afraid of being turned away.

I also know what it's like to use a fake name.

"That works," I say, keeping my tone light.

"Thanks."

Is he in some kind of trouble?

It's not my business. That's what I tell myself as I grab a set of keys from the hook behind me. Even charming old bed and breakfasts use key cards these days. It's easier to manage, for sure. My antique keys disappear with a guest every so often, despite the large wooden tag with Lighthouse Inn's logo.

"Let me show you to your room," I say, but as I move past him, I scent him. That's the only word for it. I scent him, the way a female lion might sense a male. My body becomes lithe and liquid in response. This close, I can see the shadows on the planes of his face. Broad shoulders. There's a sense that he's hunting me. Which means I'm the prey.

We stand in the small vestibule between the front desk and the door. It's too small a space for the both of us, but we breathe in those moments—in, out, in, out. I stare into eyes so dark they make me shiver. It's not just the color of them. It's the bleakness.

Then I force myself to look away. To step aside.

This man is dangerous to me.

Chapter Two

Sam

My focus should be on work.

But as I follow the pretty little innkeeper up the stairs, I can't stop admiring her gorgeous ass. It's tight and round, causing my palm to tingle with the need to touch. But I force the thoughts from my head. *No pleasure.* That's exactly what I told her, and it's what I meant. I don't get to touch her, though I can't help but look.

"How long have you worked here?" I ask with forced nonchalance.

We reach the landing, and she turns back to smile at me. "It's mine. I own it. My name is Marjorie, by the way. Marjorie Dunn."

I knew that, of course. I know so much about her she'd be terrified. She's owned the property for five years. It's the same year when she mysteriously appeared as Marjorie Dunn. There's no record of her from before that.

"A few years," she calls over her shoulder.

I follow her slowly, admiring the sight of her ass. The rest of it's lovely, too. The entire package of this woman and her quaint little inn. It feels welcoming for a stranger but still homey and lived in. A strange sensation. Most of my life has been spent in hotel rooms and safehouses. And before that, low-rent apartments devoid of affection.

"You from around here?" It's small talk. I'm interrogating her, not using torture or persuasion. No, I'm using the societal pressure of small talk.

I know what I look like. A goddamn bruiser. She's nervous being in the same room with me. The little silky hairs on the back of her neck are probably standing up. That's her instinct talking. The instinct that she's in danger.

And it's telling her the truth.

Unfortunately for her, society drills that instinct out of us.

Women, especially.

They're trained from a young age to be polite. To shove down the evolutionary knowledge that she's in the presence of a killer.

She unlocks the door with an antique brass key. "No, actually. Moved here a few years ago. I was passing through and fell in love with the town. And this house in particular. It has beautiful bones."

"Beautiful bones. That sounds… bleak."

A small smile. "It's the opposite. Beautiful bones means there's always a chance to rebuild. It means there's something worthwhile underneath the rubble. Anyway, I passed through here about five years ago. I fell in love with the town and this house."

The innocent hope in her tone is like a goddamned aphrodisiac.

I want to hear more of it.

The people who paid me want specific evidence related to her past, and her father. The night she fled with her mother must still be clear in her mind. If I'm lucky, I won't have to burrow into that pretty little head to find it. It will be here, with her. I shouldn't need torture to dig up old papers.

"What brought you all the way out here?" I set the duffle on the handscraped floor. Cream molding. Patterned wallpaper. The view through the window is exquisite, but not as beautiful as the dark-haired pixie-like woman behind me. I don't look at her, hoping it will make her feel more at ease to answer my question.

"I was… adrift," she says. "Lost for a while. I wanted a quiet life. A peaceful life." She still sounds a little lost, and instinct urges me to dig deeper. It's part of the job, I tell myself. Her father was a soldier who was killed by his crooked army men, who then framed him. Her mother took Marjorie on the run.

The pain she must have felt gives me pause, but I know I have to do this.

"Quiet is nice," I say, still keeping my expression neutral as I turn to her. Watching her toil with her words, I find myself intrigued. "Peace is nice. I'm not sure what either of those really feel like."

She's lived a quiet life ever since her mother took her.

As long as I can find what I need, she'll keep her quiet life.

Marjorie is the only person alive who could have the evidence I'm looking for. The men who hired me are concerned that it exists outside their control. They have no doubt she remembers the night they shot her father. She was there, even if she was a child. It's not something you can easily forget, they think. But, like the evidence, it could be buried deep. Nothing more than a shadow in her memory. The mind has a way of protecting itself. People have a way of protecting themselves, too.

"Breakfast is at eight o'clock usually, but since you're the only guest, I can move it if that works better for you." She continues telling me about the schedule, the amenities. There's even a goddamn bird watching journal that's used by any guest, like an ornithology guest book. It's so damn quaint it makes me itch. I don't like probing into her secrets this way, it doesn't feel right.

My orders are to find the evidence. To deceive her, if necessary.

I don't see myself ever touching her in any way that would cause pain.

But I do want to touch her. My hands itch to discover the softness of her skin. The tension in her curls. I find myself moving closer, using stealth as if I'm going to attack. She smiles up at me, her expression uncertain. That instinct again.

"Well," she says, "I think that's everything."

It should be the end, but she hands me the key to the room. I can't stop myself from brushing my fingers against hers. Heat. Electricity. Desire. It sparks where my skin touches hers. It spreads throughout my entire body, making me burn.

Those Bambi eyes look up at me, and I'm gone. Dead. Over.

Her lips part, so plump and inviting that my cock throbs against my zipper.

"I hope you enjoy your stay," she tells me softly before turning and leaving.

I let out a breath as I listen to her soft footfalls go down the stairs.

I'm fucked.

The lock on the bedroom door is flimsy. Easy to pick. Or someone could kick the door open, but I don't think my pretty little innkeeper is going to do that. Still, I grab an antique-looking chair from the wall and prop it under the knob as a safeguard. A lifetime of danger has made me cautious. Moving through the room, I check for cameras or bugs.

The room is clear.

I open the duffel bag. There are two days' worth of clothes, exactly enough for my mission here. The cash keeps anyone from finding me. Along with my service weapon.

I don't have any form of identification. It comes with the job.

I'm always someone else—never me.

When my cell phone vibrates in my pocket, I already know who it is before I look at the screen. I pull the device out and flick the answer button before pressing it to my ear. "Yeah?" My voice is low, rough. I can't afford to have her hear me talking, especially to him.

My handler is a bastard. One who will be calling every day for updates. This isn't supposed to be a high-pressure job. It's not a hit, like many others I've been tasked with. But he'll act like it is.

"Sitrep," he says without greeting me. It's not personal. Being in this line of work, there's no reason to be friendly with anyone. It's business.

"I'm going to need more time to talk to her, build up trust," I inform him. Even though I could tell him more about her, I don't. I hold back her comment about something that had happened in her past.

"Get it done," he informs me in his usual stone-cold manner.

He hangs up before I can respond.

How the fuck am I going to play this? It's true that I need a bit more time to find the evidence. And more importantly, I don't want anyone at the CIA to get any ideas about hurting her to speed up the process. If I said anything to my handler, I'd be yanked from this job so fast my head would spin. And they'd send someone else to finish the hit.

Chapter Three

I can't get Sam out of my mind. The slightest brush of his fingers along mine had my body responding in ways it hadn't done in such a long time. I needed to breathe after leaving him to settle in. The moment I walked outside, I pulled in a breath of fresh air, but still, my skin was hot where he'd touched me.

I've never had such an innate reaction to any man.

It's a solitary life. I spend my time focused on the inn, rather than making a connection to someone. The fear of losing them, having my heart broken, doesn't sit well with me. I'm more comfortable on my own. Safer, too.

I'm almost certain he'll be awake early in the morning, so I set my alarm to wake me at five. It will give me enough time to cook a full breakfast. I want to make sure he's happy and enjoys his time in my home. I know what it's like to need a haven.

It's more than my role as the innkeeper.

There's a long-dormant feminine side of me that wants to comfort him.

I head into my workroom. The half-bound book waits for me. My tools are lined up. A breath of quiet relief releases. This is why I do this. There are many things I could bind, of course. Novels. Encyclopedias. Even personal journals. I prefer to do scrapbooks. There's something beautiful about documenting the past. About embossing it and gilding it.

My small online shop accepts limited orders. I'm sent boxes of photo albums. Sometimes they come with torn ticket stubs or fading wedding invitations. Telegraphs from soldiers to their loved ones waiting at home. This is history. Permanence. This is home.

I don't have a past. No pictures. No papers. Only memories—and dark ones at that.

When I wake up in the morning, I stretch in my cotton-and-lace sheets.

My fingers are stiff from working late, but I don't regret it. The work cleared my mind.

I pull the curtain open. I'm met with a sky brilliant with color—the orange glow of sunrise meeting the sparkle of sea. It feels like we're right on the edge of the world.

A figure darkens the sand.

Male. Tall. Muscled. He runs briskly along the shoreline wearing only shorts and shoes. No shirt, even though it must be cold. I can feel the chill pressing against the glass of the window. It could be anyone, theoretically. There are other businesses. Other houses. But I know everyone in Eben Cape. And besides, this looks like the mysterious Sam Smith.

It feels like him, even though I've barely seen him. And never shirtless.

He's sweaty. Glistening. There's a rhythmic quality to his stride. It moves the muscles of his chest. My mouth becomes dry. It's rude to stare, but I can't turn away.

And so I watch until he disappears into the shoreline.

A moment passes, and I laugh at myself. *Are you so hard up for male company that you're lusting after the only single man who's presented himself?*

Sometimes the life of an innkeeper is as lonely as the one on the road.

The scrapbooking business takes a backseat to the inn. It's great for nights or days when we're vacant. I have a regular schedule for when we have guests, which includes making breakfast.

Butcher block counters and distressed blue cabinets welcome me. Between the complimentary breakfasts, optional lunches, and afternoon teas, I spend a lot of time here. The only meal I don't offer is dinner, because my talents are more about baking. I get by at lunch with sandwiches and soups. Cooking full meals is really beyond me. But I can make a delicious apricot pastry, which is a far cry from the microwave noodles I grew up with.

Ceramic canisters contain flour and sugar. I scoop them into bowls to begin cooking.

By the time I'm working in the kitchen, I hear the bell. He's back.

Footsteps on the stairs. The creak of hot water through the pipes.

My heart thumps in my chest. I finish preparing breakfast, not quite paying attention. My thumb suffers from my distraction because I burn myself. "Ouch."

I enjoy cooking. It's given me a focus when I needed it most. The inn means a lot to me. It's the only thing I own, the only thing that belongs to me in the world.

The water stops as I'm getting the serving dishes ready, so I give him some time to get dressed. With extra care, I set the table, ensuring there's enough of everything. The waffles, eggs, and bacon are still warm as I set them on the sideboard. I ended up making more than I usually do because I'm sure he'll be starving after his run.

And because he's a large man. Packed with muscle.

There's silence coming from upstairs. As the time ticks by, I'm worried the food will get cold. I leave the apron on the table and make my way to the stairs. Perhaps I should let him know everything is ready. Most guests would just come downstairs, but others will wait for me to give them a nudge.

Perhaps he's decided to give me space to get the food cooked.

With every step I take, I inhale deeply. The masculine scent of his bodywash permeates the air. It's a subtle fragrance which just makes it seem more intimate. It makes me think about him standing in the claw-foot tower under the showerhead, the way the water must have run down his abs. Heat burns my cheeks at the thought.

I step onto the landing.

The bathroom door swings open. Sam emerges from the steaming room wrapped in nothing but a towel. Every inch of his skin is dripping wet, and I can't stop my thirsty gaze from drinking in every part of him that's visible. His muscles gleam as the shimmering liquid sticks to him. Broad shoulders give way to hard-packed, muscled arms. His chest is lightly dusted with golden-brown hair.

And his abs are as chiseled as the Maine cliffside.

But what captures my attention is the prominent V which disappears beneath the towel. My throat turns dry. There's a bulge in the front of the towel, and I have to bite down on my lip to keep sounds from escaping my mouth.

We're close. Far too close on the small landing.

He takes a step toward me.

I stumble, flustered, out of breath, but before I can hit the ground, Sam catches me in his strong arms. His body is flush with mine as he pulls me against his warmth. The air is thick with steam as he stares down at me, his eyes dark.

My palms go to his chest. Those muscles? I can feel them. Mold my hands around them. Imagine him rising above me. Every part of him is hard against my body.

Desire rises in his eyes. Desire that holds me hostage for a long moment. The only sound is his breathing. And mine. And the soft *drip drip drip* of hot water falling from his body to the old hardwood floors.

"I... I made breakfast." I whisper the words in a breathy tone which has my cheeks heating once more. The man before me is like a spy out of a movie—dangerous and handsome. I don't want him to let go of me... but there's also a sense that I can't trust him.

He searches my eyes, as if he's trying to find answers. After a tense few seconds, he straightens and releases me. I shiver, already missing his heat.

"I'll be right down," he tells me in that gruff way which does something else to my body. Something I don't want to think about. I nod and turn away, putting my hand on the banister. When the click of his bedroom door sounds, I can finally breathe again.

I make my way down to the dining room.

The coffee pot is on the table, so he won't need to call on me again. Thankfully.

That was intense. I head into my workroom, hoping to give him some space to enjoy the quiet of the room. And to give myself some space, too. Except it feels strangely stuffy in here today. The day has stayed chilly, even though there is a small sliver of sunshine that's peeking through the clouds. I busy myself with the book, focusing on the tipped-in frontispiece rather than the man in my house that makes me feel things I shouldn't feel.

Chapter Four

Sam

I don't want to get closer to this woman.

I don't want to care about her.

The feel of her body against mine has imprinted in my mind. But my job is to get closer, to delve into her life. It will hurt her if she discovers what I'm doing. But there's a deeper instinct telling me to protect her.

A meal is spread out. Crisp bacon and fluffy eggs. A stack of pancakes. A carafe of orange juice that looks fresh squeezed. My stomach grumbles as if I've never eaten before in my life.

In a way, I haven't. Oh, there have been five-course meals. Expensive white plates with seared scallops and truffle sauce. The sort of thing made by chefs to sell. This isn't like that at all. It's made in someone's kitchen to nourish the people they love, like a mother makes for a child. Or a wife makes for a husband.

I bite down on a piece of sugar-dusted waffle. A reluctant rumble of appreciation vibrates through my chest. It's decadent in a way that has nothing to do with Michelin stars. Each bite warms me from the inside out.

As if she's put a bit of sunshine in the cooking.

My chest tightens at the thought of Marjorie preparing everything for me to enjoy. It causes a lump to form in my throat. *Fucking hell.* Emotions have never been an issue for me because I bury them deep–where they belong. I learned that on my first job. No, I learned that before I was even recruited into the CIA, too smart and pissed off for my own good. I'd tripped some kind of wire in the system. Athletics combined with top grades in engineering had them knocking at my door. They'd been happy to beat the salary of private firms as long as I signed my life over. It had been the easiest signature I'd ever written.

Since stepping onto Maine soil, things have been different.

It's too peaceful here. Too fucking quiet. Not the fake stillness of calm before a firefight. This is the real fucking thing with birds singing and waves lapping against stone.

I went for a run this morning to clear my head.

It didn't work. Not when I walked back into the inn, smelling sweetness and salt. And definitely not when I bumped into Marjorie on the landing, her body warm against mine.

My past has been littered with darkness and violence.

I've never had a place to call home. I didn't grow up with loving parents. My mother was a prostitute, too busy trying to get her next hit to cook dinner. My father was just one of the many customers who darkened our stoop.

Running drugs was a way to buy food and clothes. College was only possible because I was a fucking beast on the basketball court. And then the CIA found me.

I gave everything to the service. I've been shot, burned, and tortured. And I never once thought about quitting. Not until I set foot inside the Lighthouse Inn.

Marjorie walks in as I take the final bite. Her dark hair shimmers with raindrops. Her cheeks are red from the cold. She looks like some otherworldly creature. Fae or something. Not really human as she hums a greeting.

"How's breakfast?"

"Delicious. How was the cold?"

A small laugh. "Beautiful. I think some days I go outside just so I can be freezing. When I come back inside, I'm reminded of how blessed I am to have this house."

What a goddamn Pollyanna.

It's adorable. And alarming. I don't want the CIA to touch her with a ten-foot pole. Even my presence here is too close to the darkness I've seen.

"Eben Cape was started by lobstermen," she says, telling me more about the history. I wonder how much of this is part of her job as the innkeeper—and how much is her desire for permanence when her childhood was uprooted.

I can't allow myself to get emotionally entangled with her. She's nothing more than a job I have to complete. "And you've gotten to know everyone here?" I ask, just to hear her voice again.

"It's been like finding a new family." Her words are filled with sadness, causing my chest to ache from the knowledge that she's lost her real family. But each time I try to tell myself that, the more I find I want to know about her. Not because of the job. I just want to learn all there is to know about Marjorie.

"Sounds nice." The bitterness on my tongue has nothing to do with the coffee, but instead, my own history. "Sometimes the family you find is better than the one you're born with."

"Are you speaking from experience?"

"No," I say. "I haven't found family."

She gives me a small, gentle smile. "Maybe you'll find some here."

Chapter Five

Marjorie

Innkeepers keep early hours, but it's still a surprise when my phone rings at six o'clock. The phone flashes with the name *Emily Rochester*.

"Is something wrong?" It's a dramatic way to answer the phone, but I can't help it. Emily's been through hell and back, thanks to her deceased husband. She's mostly rebuilt her life. I can't help but worry. I know how hard the past holds on to you.

"No," she says quickly, sounding a little chagrined. "I'm sorry to make you worry. It's just that I got Mateo to agree to take me up the coast to that little shop. You know the one."

"The naked baby record player." We both love to go antiquing. The shop names never stick in our heads, though. Instead, we remember them by the strangest thing we've ever found in the aisles. A portrait of Elvis made entirely of seeds. A freakishly realistic mounted head of a T-rex, which must have used the skin and eyes of another poor creature. In this case, it was a gramophone with a scalloped horn, each leaf engraved with a naked, winking cherub.

"I already called, and they're open. I thought you could come."

"I have a guest," I say with some regret. Emily and I have been friends for years. She's only recently started dating the heartthrob Mateo Martin. I want her to be happy. God, she deserves it after what she's been through, but I can't help but be wary. Her first husband was abusive. I wouldn't trust any man with her right now, but she wants me to get to know him.

"But it's the off season."

"He didn't get the memo." My voice is flippant, as if it's no big deal that there's someone here. When in reality, it feels strange. Purposeful. As if he didn't just stop somewhere on his path. As if this was his destination all along. "What are you looking for?"

"There's this space at the end of the hall that needs filling." She's been methodically replacing each piece of furniture since she moved in. After the dark memories and the literal fire, she wants a fresh start for her and her adorable daughter. "But you know the best things are always surprises. Paige still loves that parking meter we found last time."

It was a birthday present for her daughter. Paige is precocious and sweet—and obsessed with all things Monopoly. We found the parking meter in the back of a shop. Emily cleaned it up and painted it red. Along the pole, she wrote *Free Parking*.

"Does Mateo like antiquing?"

"He's never been, but Paige slept over at Beau and Jane's last night. I already know she stayed up late and ate too much popcorn. So she won't come back for a couple hours."

She keeps talking about Paige and how she's getting along with Mateo.

I move the phone call to my watch so I can stick my phone in my pocket. As much as I love old things, I also embrace technology. It allows me to stay on the phone while I grab the vacuum cleaner from the closet. It's not the first time we've ever chatted while I did housekeeping. Sam went out for his morning run again today, so I'm going to tidy up before he gets back.

And hopefully avoid another awkward run-in outside the steaming bathroom.

I use my duplicate key to unlock his room and step inside. It looks tidy. Clean. It will only take a couple minutes to run through my tasks. "Keep an eye out for paper," I say.

She knows this, of course. I love to collect paper to use in my scrapbooks. Occasionally lace and other pieces. It's part of building a legacy, pulling pieces of the past together.

I give it the once-over with the Dyson before I make the bed. A flush rises in my cheeks as I imagine his body sliding between the cool sheets. The memory of this morning haunts me. Water dripped down his muscled chest. A towel was wrapped around lean hips. I can't deny that I was attracted to him. He's rugged and strong. And mysterious.

I shouldn't like a man who's mysterious.

When he pulled me into his arms, I couldn't stop my thighs from squeezing together. It's a base reaction. Unstoppable. I've never had sex with one of my guests. I've never wanted to, but I'm thinking of it now. Sam certainly has captured my attention. I'm not sure that's a good thing since I don't know anything about him.

I turn down the coverlet. As I do, I bump the duffel bag. It's sitting on the chair at the foot of the bed. My elbow hits something hard. It could be any number of things. A book. A laptop. Lots of things are hard, but suspicion tightens my throat.

My guests deserve privacy.

No, I've never once encroached on anyone's luggage, or their personal belongings, but there's something off about Sam. And deep down, even though I've tried to bury it deep, that niggling feeling continues to plague me. I just can't force it down.

Sam Smith.

There's a decent chance it's a fake name, especially since he paid cash. Which just begs the question—what is he doing here? It's been running through my mind all day.

He told me he was here on business, but he hasn't even asked for the Wi-Fi password. Everyone does that, even when they're on vacation. And that makes me nervous.

The zipper on his black duffel bag is half open. That's a good thing, right? It means he has nothing to hide. And it's not really snooping if I move so I can see further inside. Crisp white dress shirts sit on top of black pants. A black leather wallet that looks thicker than usual. In fact, it reminds me of the badge I used to play with as a child. My father's badge.

"What's wrong?" Emily's voice sounds far away.

My heart hammers in my chest as I stare down at it, the smooth black leather and the hint of gold peeking from the side. It could mean anything, of course. He could be a cop or a soldier. Lots of places have badges. It could even be pretend, though the idea of this man playing any sort of game feels all wrong. He's serious. Completely serious.

"Marjorie?"

And even if he is CIA, that doesn't mean he has any connection to my father. It doesn't mean he has any connection to what happened over a decade ago.

Fear races through me, every nerve in my body is alight with it, and I can't stop my hands from trembling as anxiety twists in my gut. "It's nothing," I say through the knot in my throat. "Nothing. I just... realized

I forgot to start breakfast. I've got to go."

I stumble backward as the past and present seem to twine around each other. Flashes spark in the back of my lids each time I blink. My chest tightens as panic sets in. I remember the glint of a black barrel. A gun pointed at my father.

For a moment, I'm a child again. My father shouts at me to run. I ran to the attic and locked myself inside. I cried until my tears were dry and sticky on my cheeks.

After a long while, my mother came back.

We went on the run. It was the only way we could survive.

All those times Mom held me close as I woke from nightmares, she questioned me time and time again, but I told her I didn't remember. She took me to therapists. I sat in their offices for hours while they tried to delve into my mind.

I lied to all of them.

I told them I had blocked whatever it was out of my mind. I told them I didn't remember the most terrifying night of my life. They all stared at me as if I was a poor girl who had lost her father. None of them forced me, though.

I stood by my story—*I don't remember.*

But the truth is, I do.

I can recall that night as if it were happening right in front of me. I don't know why I couldn't bring myself to admit it, but I never wanted to talk about it again. And each time someone asked me about it, I found it easier to tell them the lie I made up.

None of that matters now. I shake my head, hard. Breakfast. That's what I told Emily, and I meant it. I need to start breakfast. Food for the mysterious guest with a CIA badge in his bag. I back out of the room and head for the stairs.

Chapter Six

Sam

It's too peaceful at the Lighthouse Inn. Marjorie's built the place up to be a haven, a place to rest. It's a collection of quiet, sunny spaces.

Which makes it impossible not to notice her.

Noticing is the job. Finding evidence is the reason I'm here.

But sensing every breath she takes? Every light step across the floor? Every sway of her hips? One creak of the stairs, and my mind plays out a hundred filthy scenarios. All of them end with her naked. Only the location changes. The kitchen. The room upstairs with its flimsy lock.

The carefully maintained furniture in the living room.

I'd make her feel good. Make that otherworldly face pink with pleasure.

That's not the job, and I damn well know it.

Wind and waves do a decent job of clearing my mind. Caring about Marjorie the innkeeper is not my first priority. Completing my mission is my first and only priority.

The man I am? He doesn't make plans.

He doesn't have a future.

I kick the sand off my shoes on a mat by the back door and slip inside.

Marjorie's upstairs. I can hear her voice. Must be on the phone. Her footsteps move back and forth.

I've been here long enough to know that she doesn't keep anything in plain sight. The living room's cozy, with throw pillows and blankets and a small collection of books. It's not cluttered. I've poked my head in everywhere except one room.

When I'm sure she's settled in, her footsteps going back and forth, I move carefully to a closed door near the dining room.

I'm only here to surveil it. Determine if I'll need to pick the lock. The hardware on the door is about the same quality as the rooms upstairs. I'm expecting this to need a key, since it's been shut tight the whole time I've been here.

Instead, the knob turns under my hand. The door swings open to reveal a workspace. Marjorie keeps it neat, just like the rest of the inn, but there's more.

A big worktable has a low stack of boxes on one end. A scrapbook is opened in the center of the table. A small lamp perches in the corner. A few paper organizers, stacked side-by-side, line the walls. A wire rack holds a variety of scissors.

Scrapbooking?

It strikes me as an odd hobby for a woman who only popped into existence five years ago. But when I lean over the table to see the open pages, none of them have to do with Marjorie.

The people in the photos look nothing like her. A newspaper clipping lined up next to the books has a photo of the same people with their names printed underneath. Howard Forsyth and his wife, Carol. I scan the area again. There's a handwritten note tacked to the wall.

Thank you so much for doing this. It means a lot to our family. Can't wait to see the results!

—Evelyn Forsyth

Who ever heard of making scrapbooks for other people? Though, if I think about it… maybe it's the perfect hobby for a person like Marjorie. These scrapbooks must be new families for her just like the visitors at the inn. A sweet kind of wish fulfillment. From the way she spoke about family, it's clear she wished she had one. In this workroom, she takes bits of the past and gives them pleasing arrangements on the page. It tugs at my heart to think of her in here with her head bowed over the history of someone else's love.

I clear my throat and push that emotion down. Work has never been about emotion. If it was, I'd never have survived the shit that usually comes with my assignments. Long nights in enemy territory. Hours of what the government likes to call "enhanced interrogation." Years without a home or a family.

Those things aren't the end goal, either. The end goal is just to make it out. An operative doesn't think beyond the conclusion of an assignment, even if it's the last one. He doesn't make plans.

The scrapbook isn't the only thing in the room. Two file cabinets against the wall are the most likely place to find paperwork about Marjorie's father.

And if I find the evidence now, I can spend the rest of the time…

What?

Being with her?

That's hardly an option. If I find it right now, the only choice is to leave. Walk straight out the front door. All the things in my duffel bag can be replaced.

I pull open one of the doors on the filing cabinet. This is one of the better things I've done in my line of work. It doesn't involve bodily injury or torture of the mind. It's a search mission. The cabinet is filled with folders, each labeled with handwriting I recognize from the second column in her ledger.

It's her. This is what she's been doing. Her recent past. All that exists, if the records are to be believed. She came into existence five years ago, and all the proof is here.

I want to know about her.

I want to read every file in this cabinet. Assemble them like the pages of her scrapbook. If she made that into a book, I'd read it every night.

I recognize that urge for what it is—a fucking problem. Entanglement like this is not for a man like me. Not now. Not ever. I pull the folders apart methodically. Records from her Etsy business. Invoices. Notes from customers. One folder is thicker than the others. I ease it open with a fingertip and find a sealed packing envelope inside. It's heavy.

A returned scrapbook.

"What are you doing in here?"

How the fuck did I not hear her? I keep my heartbeat steady out of habit, but I'm caught. Red-handed. I put both palms out in front of me, where she can see them. Marjorie stands in the doorway. Her face is pale. Eyes wide.

"I was curious." I go for a smile, but she doesn't smile back. "It's an intriguing little room you have here."

She swallows hard. "I saw your gun upstairs."

Okay. I'll need another approach.

"Marjorie—"

"Why do you have a gun?" She huffs out a breath and holds her body still. I can see how much she wants to run. "Are you police? CIA?"

I let my hands down. Let out my own breath. She needs to see me as calm. As calm as a man like me can look. "CIA."

Marjorie's eyes go from me to the filing cabinet. "I'm pretty sure there's nothing in there for you."

"No." I push a hand through my hair. It's an imitation of exasperation, but real frustration pushes at my chest. "There's nothing. My career's given me a nasty habit."

"A habit?" Suspicion darkens her eyes along with curiosity.

"I have this drive to find information. To… uncover." Marjorie watches me, her body angled slightly away. But she hasn't left the room yet. She hasn't run away, which would be a damned shame. "I can't help it. Even in a place like this."

She worries at her lip with her teeth. "That's really strange, Sam."

"It's terrible. That's what it is."

"I don't know about that."

"I do. I hate it. I've hated it for years. The CIA made me into this person early on, but it's not who I wanted to be. Some asshole looking through your filing cabinets—Jesus."

Marjorie takes a small step into the room. "You didn't do any harm," she offers. I hate that I'm doing this to her. Hate it. She's still trying to play the role of the innkeeper. Keeping the peace when I don't deserve it. "It's just scrapbooking stuff."

"You don't have to lie to me." I'm lying to her. It's just another day on the job. Lying through my teeth. Pretending to be a man I don't want to be. "You were all pale when you came in here. The gun scared you."

"Yeah," she admits in a soft voice. "It did." Marjorie's skin stays slightly pale.

The pretty little innkeeper looks small. Alone.

"I'm sorry you came across it that way." I open my arms wide. Two reasons. One, to offer her a goddamn hug, like a civilized person and not a murder for hire. Two—to show her I don't have another gun at my waist.

Marjorie looks for it.

There's nothing there. I didn't carry anything with me for my run.

A couple seconds of hesitation, and she rushes across the room and tucks herself into my arms.

Chapter Seven

Marjorie

The warmth of him calms me in spite of myself.

No part of me should want to be near Sam. He's going through my things, searching for something in a room I never gave him permission to be in. He did this on purpose. Sam waited until he thought I was distracted to come in here.

My heart pounds. A CIA agent at the inn can't mean anything good. But his strong arms wrapped around me and the masculine scent of him battle against my fear.

He feels good.

He looks even better. It was a mistake, ever allowing myself to be attracted to this muscled, dangerous man.

Sam is not bothered by my fear. His heart hasn't picked up speed. He's steady. "You're okay," he says.

"I'm not. And I think you should leave. You were going through my things." They're not even my things, really. I don't have much from my old life in the filing cabinets. It's mostly business records and a scrapbook that was returned to me in the mail. I never heard from that family again. Maybe they had to disappear because a man like Sam showed up at their house before they could accept the delivery.

He creates space between us so he can look into my eyes. Sam looks into them like he's finding more information there. I don't really want to give it to him. "Listen. I'm not going to hurt you, Marjorie. There's no need to be afraid."

The cold fear in my veins reminds me of everything I've tried to forget. Everything I've tried to keep locked outside. The Lighthouse Inn is a boundary between me and my past. I've worked hard to make it peaceful and light. It's never dark. Never terrifying. That's the experience I offer to my guests.

Sam is trying to give it to me. That's what it seems like. But how could he when he's the one who stuck into my workroom?

"You don't have to be afraid. I was an asshole, but you're not in danger."

I want to say that I don't believe him. Except he hasn't asked me to. That, more than anything, makes me believe him. The sound of his voice soothes me. I know I shouldn't want to be soothed, and not by him, but he's warm and confident. "I'm afraid."

"I understand." He keeps his voice low and his palms steady on my back.

Those two words are proof of his experience. The way he says it makes me think he knows.

He does.

Sam is running from violence, too. A dark life. A risky one. And what he found when he stepped into my inn was solace. This is a safe harbor for him, just like it is for me.

Which is what I intended all along. I wanted to make a safe, comfortable place for people. I just never meant to invite danger into it.

The truth is that I want safe harbor, too. I'm shaken by the sight of him in here. The inn itself can't give me that safe harbor. All of my antiques and all of my routines can't give that to me.

It's not enough for this moment.

The only safe harbor I want is in another person. In Sam.

I tilt my face up to his. It's a test. If he can kiss me like he's safe, maybe I can settle down. Stop being so fucking afraid.

Sam hesitates, his dark eyes searching mine. They glint with how much he wants this. The smallest tension in his muscles gives him away. *Prove it*, I'm saying with my invitation. *Prove you won't hurt me. Prove you were telling the truth.*

He bends his head to mine with a frustrated groan. In that sound, I hear how he's been holding himself back. Maybe for as long as I have. Since he first walked in the door of the inn.

Sam's mouth meets mine in a rough, possessive crash. It's the kiss of a man who's finished resisting. Who's constantly having to restrain himself, and now he can't anymore. He makes a low noise and pulls back. He takes a sharp breath, but that's all the control he has.

He kisses me again. Hard. I can't help but like this about him. He might have given me a fake name, but this is his real kiss. This is the real man.

I want more of him.

It's against every instinct that's kept me safe all these years, but it's so powerful that it feels like a storm off the ocean. It's ready to shake down the walls of the inn. Only it's me shaking, not the foundation.

I press my body harder into his, throw my arms around his neck, and beg him silently to take me upstairs. If Sam pushes me away, if he turns his back—

He doesn't.

He takes me into his arms, lifting me from the floor without a hint of effort, and goes up the stairs. In his guest room, he puts me on my feet and strips off my clothes. Sam's matter-of-fact about it. He does the same to his own clothes, tossing them to the floor in a pile that somehow remains neat.

Then he's all motion and muscle, taking me to the bed and spreading me out. His body folds over mine. Sam crushes more rough kisses to my lips. More and more and more until I feel like I'm part of the bedspread. Until I'm melted electricity, waiting for him. He eases my thighs apart with his body, kissing me with the same kind of thorough concentration he was using to go through my things.

He kisses me like he's discovering me.

Like I'm all the information he could ever need.

Like his last job is to kiss me in a way I'll never forget.

Sam runs callused palms over every inch of my body. Testing my skin. Exploring it. Finding something there. I'm not sure there's anything to find. I've never been a very interesting person. And now I'm Marjorie Dunn. A boring, safe name for a boring, safe life. A life where nothing ever gets dark. A life where nothing ever comes to the door and sends you fleeing to the attic.

There's no mystery here, but Sam acts like I'm the greatest mystery of his life. Of anyone's life. He's thick and hard between my legs, and I want him inside me.

No more waiting.

I angle myself up toward him, and he pushes inside with a shudder. It forces a relieved breath out of my lungs. It's been so long since I had a man in my bed. The moment he seats himself, I know. This is what I've needed. I wanted this the second I saw him. He stretches me, but our bodies fit together like they're part of a set. I'm wet for him.

We move together. It's a dark, thoughtless movement, but he doesn't seem like a stranger. This doesn't feel like hiding.

Sam needs this from me as much as I need it from him.

He buries his face in my neck and fucks me like he'll never have another chance. If this is his last assignment, he's going to drink it in. His lips trail over my skin. He inhales and grunts with a feral abandon while he strokes, again and again and again, using my body for his pleasure.

I'm lost in him when he pulls back, gritting his teeth. His hand works between us. This is hard, hot sex, but he doesn't want me to be without pleasure. His knuckles graze my clit. They keep moving. Keep circling.

"Come on," he urges. "Come on, Marjorie. Let me make you feel good."

The sensation he coaxes out of my oversensitive nerves feels so good that it sends me flying. Away from the inn. Away from my past. Away from the fear I felt. Everything melts away except the movement of his fingers over my body.

This is the only place I ever want to be for the rest of my life. What could ever convince me to leave?

Pleasure ripples out over me. It takes me in its hands and squeezes, pulsing until it shakes my body around the thick intrusion of him. Until Sam's moving with me in that pleasure and fighting for his own.

His body tenses, and he comes with an animal sound. I feel like it's been pent up inside him for years and years. He's been craving this. He needs this. He might die without the touch of another person. Without being inside me.

I hook my fingertips into his back and hold him while he shudders out all that pleasure. When he's finished, he rests his head against me, breathing hard.

I don't think this is normal. He's so strong. It can't possibly have been too much for him. It feels monumental, though. My skin is all tingly with the aftershocks. My whole body is awake with how intimate this is.

"That was good," I murmur into his ear, looping my arms around his neck.

"Thank god," he says. "Thank god."

He was pretending. Pretending to be calm and sure and confident. He didn't know if I would like this, and he's relieved.

Sam's found a kind of solace.

He's safe.

I'm just not sure if I am.

Chapter Eight

Sam

I can't bring myself to leave her alone in the bed.

When Marjorie falls asleep, I lay my head on the pillow and sleep next to her. I want to be near her so much that it overrides all my years of training and knocks down my commitment to detachment. I could try to justify it to myself by saying it's about getting closer to her. That it's about reducing her fear so I'll have more time to hunt down the evidence. That it's about the job and nothing else, but it's not.

That's bullshit.

I just want to be near her. I want her body folded against mine. I want to hear every peaceful breath. I want to breathe her in the whole damn night.

And the next night. Every night.

Being in bed with her makes me imagine a future outside the CIA. That's not an option for me. It hasn't been an option since the day I signed on the dotted line. A contract like mine is for life. Once in a while, an agent retires, but for what? You'd always be looking over your shoulder. I knew what I was giving up when I signed on. By the time I'm ready to hand in my weapon, it'll be too late for a regular life as a civilian.

Despite all that, I fall asleep fast and hard next to Marjorie.

In the morning, I wake up to find her still pressed close to me. Her body has molded itself to mine. The pretty little innkeeper sleeps comfortably in the warmth I've created for her. The sun creeps up over the horizon. Any other day, I'd be out of bed the minute my eyes open. A run, a shower. My routine doesn't break for anything.

I'm not ending this a second early.

It's not long before Marjorie stirs. She comes out of sleep slowly. Stretching. Sighing. Her body presses against mine. I run my palm over her stomach to let her know I'm awake, too.

She turns over onto her back, dragging her hand over her eyes, and looks into mine. "Hi."

"Good morning."

Her gaze travels down over my chest. My stomach. The job has decorated me with marks over the years. Patches of skin that won't be quite the same. Burn marks that never faded. More than a few scars. It feels like she's rifling through all my secrets, the way I was doing to her.

Marjorie raises a fingertip and traces it over my chest.

Her touch fills me with warmth. It shouldn't. It's not secrets she's seeing, I insist to myself. It's just my track record on the job. This is the path the rest of my life will take. It'll involve more skin damage at the very least. That much is a given.

She brushes her fingertip over a red half-moon scar near my ribs.

"A job in the Middle East."

"Were you in a fight?" she murmurs.

"I saw it coming but decided to take the wound rather than blow my cover."

There are more scars for her to discover. She grazes one of them with her nail. "And this one?"

"Paris." I shift closer to her. "This is pretty one-sided. I want to know about you."

A soft laugh escapes her. Marjorie must believe there's nothing to know about her. It's bullshit. She has one hell of a history, but more than that, she has a present. A life. It's fascinating in a way I never expected. I memorize her touch while I wait for the answer. It's the question I was supposed to ask, but I didn't do it to impress my handler or wrap things up here.

I did it because I want to know.

Damn it, I want to know.

"I don't have any scars," she says.

I arch an eyebrow at her.

She laughs. "Fine. I miss…" Her gaze goes thoughtful, and I feel like a goddamn asshole. She's going to answer me honestly. She's going to give me this piece of herself after I've already searched through her background. I've read every file that exists on Marjorie Dunn. This will only flesh out those details. "I miss my dad."

"What about him?"

"He's been gone a long time." The corners of her mouth turn down. "I barely have any memories left, but I still miss him so much. Maybe what I miss is the idea of being together. And I miss…" Marjorie looks away, toward the window. The brightening sun glows on her face. "I miss how my mother would work so hard for us. She put everything she had into keeping us safe and happy, right up until she died."

"How did she die?"

I already know. Marjorie's eyes flick to mine. My chest squeezes with guilt. "Cancer. There are a lot of bad things in the world, but watching somebody die of cancer…" A quick shake of her head. "It was awful. Aside from losing my dad, it was the worst thing."

To hear this in her voice makes me question everything. Why the hell did I go into this career? Why have I stayed so long? What am I doing here? I've had a hundred conversations like this over the years. Maybe thousands. Hearing about Marjorie's past in her voice is different. Seeing her emotions cross her face, pink and warm from sleeping with me, should be against some regulation. It hurts. The pain surprises me. I'm not used to feeling anything about a job.

"Do you really hate it?" she asks. "Your work."

My base instinct is to avoid the topic, but it'll only draw more attention to this fact about me. It'll only make me seem more ominous. "For a long time, it was all I had. I don't mind the work. It's like any other job. Maybe more dangerous. It's the person I've become that I don't recognize."

It's true, goddamn it. My younger self would be horrified to discover what I've made of my life. That I'm a man who scares innocent people. Who lies to them. Who hurts them. And then, when the job's done, I walk away like it never happened. There's no reward for all this. No sense of accomplishment. I'll do this until I'm killed in the line of duty or until I can't take it anymore, and then I'll have nothing.

"What did you want to be when you grew up?"

Not this. "I went to school for engineering."

"Because you wanted to be an engineer?"

"No. I got in on a scholarship. A guidance counselor suggested engineering. I didn't know what else to do."

"What kind of scholarship?"

"Basketball."

Marjorie's eyes light up. "You played basketball?"

"What, you like sports?"

"I like how it looks when all the people on the team are working together," Marjorie admits. "There's a kind of magic in that, don't you think?"

There was. I haven't been on that kind of team since I graduated. I'm only in contact with one or two other people at a time. The CIA contract doesn't seem like a prize anymore. A life of loneliness and violence, followed by more loneliness. Death, at some point or another.

"Tell me more about you, Marjorie Dunn."

"I like it here in Eben Cape." She watches me carefully as she says this. Worried I might reject this idea, maybe. But hell. It's nice here. It could be a home. "I tried to make a life that my parents would have been proud of. They probably never imagined I'd own an inn, but they'd like it here, I think. They'd think it was peaceful. They'd understand wanting to live in a small town. It's beautiful, even in the winter. It's calm. No monsters lurking in the shadows, except…"

"Except?"

Her brow furrows. "No place is perfect. I've met some men here who made life difficult. My friend Emily's husband was one of those. He's gone now."

"Because of you?"

She snorts. "No. He got into an argument with her brother, and he was killed. It was the talk of the town last year. Made me nervous to think about people killing each other. I didn't like that. I was relieved when things quieted down. Relieved for Emily, especially." Marjorie finds another one of my scars and focuses on it. "Do the scars still bother you?"

"No." It's tough to get closer to her, but I manage another inch. "That's the thing about scars. They grow over with tissue that doesn't have nerve endings. They don't feel any pain. They're basically dead."

"It is a little like death," she agrees. "But you're still alive."

"The scars will be with me forever. Same with the hidden ones. Those wounds are covered in the same scar tissue. I don't feel anything."

That's what I've told myself for years. It's bullshit. I feel things looking into Marjorie's eyes. It's bullshit for her, too. Her wounds are there in her heart. She's built this inn as a guard for them, and she's been doing a damn good job.

"I wish I felt less sometimes. You know…" Another thoughtful sigh.

"I've made a home here, but it's not the same. Nobody ever stays for long. Maybe that's just how life is."

The promise is on my lips. *I won't leave.*

But of course I will.

That's the job.

That's my life.

It's not going to happen this minute, though. Not in the next hour. Not even today. Fuck it. I'm staying with her at least for today. I let myself indulge in the fantasy. I normally don't do that. Imagination can keep you alive through a dark night, but this isn't about imagination. It's about being in this moment.

I fold my arms around the beautiful innkeeper in my bed. "Tell me more."

"There's nothing else. I have a boring life. I walk on the beach. I make scrapbooks. I go antiquing with my friends. That's all I do. That, and the inn."

"What do you look for in those shops?"

"I like the little things." Her eyes brighten. "The things people saved for a long time. Pretty things for the shelf. Those tell you exactly what they loved. That's what I look for in antique shops. What about you?"

"I've never been," I tell her. I've never thought for a second about what I might like to keep with me. It's always a nondescript duffel bag that belongs to a man who doesn't exist.

"You should go," she says. I'd go with her. I'd go to a million antique shops and watch her face light up. "You can see so many ideas there. So many ways people made their houses into homes."

"I wouldn't know anything about that." Nothing in my life would generate a family heirloom or an antique."

"You can learn." Marjorie smiles. "I did."

Chapter Nine

Marjorie

It's no use pretending that Sam is an ordinary guest. We slept together. It was good. More than good. It makes me blush to think about it. Letting a man have sex with me is so far outside the norm that my skin hums even after he climbs out of bed.

Sam's still in the shower when I'm finished with mine. I dry my hair, dress for the day, and go down to the kitchen.

Making him breakfast like usual feels disingenuous, almost. What happened between us was special. I don't want him to think it was nothing. At the same time, I don't want him to think it was everything.

We both need some fresh air. That's what I know. And—I recognized the hurt in Sam's voice when he spoke about his work, and even about the antique shop. Not knowing anything about making a home.

What do people with homes do? They make plans for the day. They go out by the beach. They're comfortable.

So I get out my big picnic basket from the pantry and open it up. I'm folding a blanket over the food I've gathered when Sam appears in the doorway. "Do you have a date?" he asks.

"We're having a picnic," I announce. "It's late enough for it to be lunch, I suppose." My face heats with how good he looks. Fitted, nondescript clothes, but the man—I could never forget the man, no matter how plainly he dressed. His body was over mine in bed last night. His hands on my skin. His mouth on my mouth. He tasted so good he'll follow me into my dreams. "You might want a coat. It's a little chilly out."

Sam returns with his jacket and mine. He helps me into mine before he puts on his own, then takes the handle of the basket in one large hand

and carries it out toward the shore.

We go some distance down the shore to a rocky cove. Other people have been here before. There are ashes from old fires. I spread the picnic blanket near the cove. Sam walks slowly down the beach, gathering branches, and I unpack the basket.

He's not gone long. A few minutes at most. It takes him even less time to start a fire.

"How did you do that? It's so windy." The wind keeps sending my hair flying into my face. I keep pushing it back, again and again.

Sam looks at me over the new flames flickering beneath his hands. "I'm good with wood."

"You're good with other things, too." He grins, and that makes my face hotter than any fire. "But—come eat. I packed a lot of food."

He takes a seat next to me on the picnic blanket. "Sandwiches?"

"Yes. I have three different kinds, depending on what you like."

"You had time to make three kinds of sandwiches?"

"You were busy." In the shower. Thinking of him naked makes me forget the wind. Forget the chill. Forget everything but the feeling of him moving over me in the bed. "Lots of guests have a more relaxed schedule when they're getting ready. I'm not saying—" I laugh out loud. "I'm just saying, you must have needed the hot water."

"I did," he agrees. "Made it easier to stay out of bed."

With me. He wanted to go back to bed with me. I wanted that, too. If he picked me up in his arms and took me inside right now, I don't think I'd disagree. Honestly? I wouldn't even need to go inside.

I take a long, slow breath and let it out. He's attractive, that's all. It's a crush. I like the sound of his voice. It doesn't mean my emotions are getting the better of me. It'll be best if I just live in the moment with him. And this moment is about sandwiches, not sex.

"A BLT." I hold up the first one. "I also have pulled pork and grilled chicken."

"Which one's your favorite?"

"The chicken is really good."

"The BLT, then."

I have cans of sparkling water and buttery crackers and purple grapes. Sam seems surprised with everything I pull out of the basket. A little thrilled, like no one has ever made a picnic for him.

It feels good to be the one to do it. Good, and… sad. I'm sad that he hates his work. That he feels like it turned him into a person he doesn't know. That nobody ever packed a picnic for him until today.

And sad that he's not the kind of man who could stay with me, even if he wanted to. A CIA agent would never have a future in Eben Cape.

But if he did, this is what it could look like. Picnics on the beach. Waking up in the morning together. Talking about the wind, and the trees, and the sand. A ship goes by out in the distance. Sam's eyes track it while he eats his sandwich.

"What do you work on in that little room?" I'm surprised to feel relief at the question. At least we won't have to pretend he wasn't in there. That would be as hard as pretending last night didn't happen. "I saw old photos. They didn't seem to be from your family."

"They weren't. I make scrapbooks for people in my spare time."

He stares out at the ocean, thinking. "They don't want to do that for themselves?"

"Some people probably do. But other people… I don't know. They don't have the time to create the books, or they're afraid it might not turn out."

Sam meets my eyes, and it sends heat through my body. He's a cold man. Dangerous. Scary. But when he looks at me like this, all I can feel is the safe cocoon of his arms. "It seems like you'd have plenty of visitors at a place like this."

"Oh, I do. Summer especially. I have more time in the off-season, but I like to keep a steady cash flow, and—" It just seems worthless to keep pretending with him. We are pretending. I know that. He's pretending not to be dangerous, and I'm pretending I have no feelings about him. "The truth is, it's not about the money. I love doing it."

"Rooting through other people's memories?" He gives me a rueful smile.

"They send them to me in the hopes I'll be able to make something beautiful. Scrapbooks like that—they're not meant to end up in secondhand stores. They're for families to pass down over the years. I'm glad to have a glimpse into what that looks like."

"Do you have one for yourself?"

I think about this question every time I start on a new project. Every time I send one off in the mail with certified tracking so it won't get lost on the way back home. I don't know what I'd put in a scrapbook. I barely have anything from my childhood. No newspaper clippings. No photos. Most of the families I make the books for have mementos from holidays. They're usually pictures taken with a blinding flash from a makeshift tripod, people crowded in front of the camera.

"Maybe I'm one of those people who's afraid to screw it up." I smile at him to make it seem true. I don't know if Sam believes me. "Someday I'll make one."

"I'd have thought you'd do your own for practice."

"I've done a couple for the inn over the years. Sometimes guests give me copies of their pictures."

"If you made one for yourself, what would you put in there?"

I lift two brownies wrapped in a kitchen towel out of the basket and give one to Sam. I don't want to admit out loud that I don't have enough for a scrapbook. In all my life, I've never had enough for a full book. But I can imagine, can't I? This picnic is an imaginary version of a life we could have.

"I'd put a photo of the first house I remember living in." Before those men came to hurt my father. Before my mother and I ran. "My parents were proud of it, I think. A photo of them standing outside. Some of my work from school. I was always proud of my handwriting. I'd definitely want quite a few items from the inn. The document from when I registered it as my own business in Eben Cape. I think I have the first dollar I accepted in cash somewhere."

"You could make a whole book about how this place looks through the seasons," Sam says. But he's not looking at the ocean, which captures everyone's attention. "I'd read a book like that if you kept it on the front desk."

"Really? Wouldn't you want to feel like the inn... I don't know. Came into being just for you and disappeared as soon as you left? Your own secret place?"

He shakes his head. "I'd want to know it was here all the time. I'd want to know how it looked in the early spring and the dead of winter and on those days in August where it's too hot to breathe."

My heart races. He could have all those things if he stayed. I wouldn't throw him out. It's a dangerous thought to have. I know that. But isn't that the point of being an innkeeper? Offering people a temporary home?

"It would be hard to take a picture if it was that hot." As hot as I feel now, even with the cold air coming in off the ocean. "I'd spend all my time in the water."

Sam smiles. "I'd like to see that, too."

Chapter Ten

Sam

I didn't know I needed a picnic.

How would I have known that? No woman has ever stood in the kitchen with light in her eyes and quick hands, putting together a basket of food. No woman has ever put a blanket on the ground and offered me a fucking sandwich, and then talked to me like...

Like it was a date.

A real date. Not an interrogation. Two people spending time with each other like they were comfortable. Like they were at home.

Marjorie's cheeks are pink from the cold by the time I help her pack up the remains of the meal and carry the basket down the beach with her. My chest aches with how much I liked that. It was simple. It was domestic and sweet and all the things I've never even hoped for.

This life—that's what I need. How could I not have seen that before? Small, easy comforts and love. Somebody packing a fucking picnic basket. I need it so much it hurts.

More than that, I feel close to her. Marjorie puts her hand on my arm as we make our way across the yard behind the inn. It feels right to steady her. It feels right to be the one she's touching.

Which is why we need distance.

I can't feel this close to her. I get attached, and that's it. That's my whole damn career, up in flames. An agent goes soft and he's not an agent anymore. He can try to hide it, but it'll all fall apart eventually. An agent with a heart can't withstand interrogation. They struggle to do what's necessary for the assignment.

I separate myself from her for hours. Through the early afternoon. Marjorie moves around the inn. She tidies. She brings me coffee. She spends a quiet stretch in her workroom.

Every move she makes shifts the space around us. It pulls my heart toward her. I've never wanted to scare Marjorie, but as the minutes pass, my resolve weakens. I need her, and I need her to understand that I'm not good for her. I'm not the man she should pack a picnic for.

I wait until I can hear her packing up. Quicker, more precise movements. A drawer opening and shutting. At the door to the workroom, I stand in the frame and watch her until she notices me with a startle.

Marjorie's hand flies to her chest. "Sam. You scared me."

"You shouldn't have let me in."

She blinks, a nervous laugh escaping her. "What do you mean? You're a guest."

"I'm not a guest, and you know it. I'm a dangerous man. And now I'm inside with you."

"I—" Her eyes move up and down my body, but she doesn't take a step back. The pretty little innkeeper doesn't try to run. Her cheeks flush. "I hope you won't hurt me."

I haven't hurt her. I'm trying to tell her that I could. I'm capable of it. I've hurt so many people before.

"What will you trade?"

Marjorie Dunn is the most beautiful person I've ever seen. I'm struck by the color of her eyes in the lamplight from her worktable. "Trade?"

"For your safety. You'll have to buy it from me."

"I don't—I don't—" She's never played a game like this before. That much is clear. "I don't have very much money. I don't have anything to offer."

"Money is nothing to me." Two quick steps and I have her wrist in my hand. She gasps. "Come upstairs and show me how much you want to live."

She barely resists on the trip up the stairs, but her eyes are wide when I back her into my bedroom. "Please. You don't have to do this."

"This is what I do. Take off your clothes."

Her hands shake, but there's no terror in Marjorie's eyes. The clothes come off in layers. She looks so sweet like this, stepping out of a pair of pants. Dropping a bra to the floor. Every curve of her skin that she exposes lights another part on fire.

I go to her when she's naked. I put my hand on her chin, force her head up, and kiss her hard. Rough. Harder than I've kissed her before. I haven't touched Marjorie Dunn like this even once. I'm expecting for her to hate it. For her to jerk away. For her to resist me.

But instead, she makes a hot begging sound into my mouth.

No. No. She's supposed to see me for what I am, and she's not.

"That's not enough." I turn her around and force her onto the bed, pinning her with my body. She bends for me even while she pants and gasps, her fear rising. I push her head to the comforter and yank her hips up into position. "You want to live?"

"Yes." Her hands clench on the fabric. "Please, yes."

"You'd offer me your pussy in exchange for your life?"

"Please, take it."

I take out my cock and find her opening. Waiting is too damn hard. I'm all pissed-off want and emotion. I'm nothing like the man I'm supposed to be. I enter her in a single stroke. Marjorie cries out at the invasion, but she pulses around me. She's fucking welcoming me, even now.

"Work for it," I order her. "Work for this. This is your fucking life, and I'm not satisfied."

She moves her hips back against me. It's hard, the way I have her pinned. I'm holding her down. Being a monster. Marjorie moans, and it almost undoes me. I stroke into her again. Hard. Fast. No consideration for her.

"Please," she begs. "Please, don't hurt me."

I pull out, turn her over, and put her wrists over her head. She squirms against my grip, fighting. "You're not giving me enough."

Marjorie opens her thighs for me, breathing hard. "Here. Here. Anything you want."

It's nothing to drive back into her. She's wet for me. It still knocks the wind out of her. "I want you to convince me."

"Convince you of what?"

That I could stay here without ruining your life. That a man like me isn't too much for a sweet little innkeeper like you. That I'm not the monster I know I've become.

"Show me how much you like it, Marjorie. Show me how much you like getting fucked by a man who wants to hurt you."

Her muscles clench around me, and her lips part. "I do."

"Don't tell me. Show me. Come on my thick cock."

"But you're—you're fucking me so hard."

I am. It's true. I can't slow the rhythm of my hips down. It feels too good to be inside her. It feels like a release from all that fucked-up feeling earlier. She's slick and hot and fitted to me exactly. I've never thought of sex as a means to get closer to a person. Not in any genuine way. It was only ever a tool to manipulate women. But I don't want to manipulate her now. I want her to see me. I want her to love me.

Oh, fuck.

"I am fucking you hard," I agree with her, my ab muscles bunching. It's hard not to come. "I don't care if it hurts. Come on my cock. You look so pretty this way, Marjorie. I wouldn't want to have to damage you."

She pulls at my hand around her wrists, trying to get free. I don't think she's actually attempting to escape. I think she's looking for pressure and contact, the way I am. Fucking hell. I did this to put distance between us, but I've never felt closer to another person. Her body is pressed all along mine, anywhere she can reach. Her sweet thighs lock around my hips.

"What will you do if I don't come?"

"Punish you for being so goddamn beautiful. I'd fuck you in all your holes. I'd make you cry with my cock down your throat. I'd put you on your knees and pull your hair and make you take it until you scratched me to get me to stop."

Her breathing picks up and up and up, her body heating around me. Marjorie's hips move faster. Jerky. It's the threats that are turning her on. They're making her wetter and tighter. She grinds herself shamelessly into me from underneath.

"I'd watch you cry," I say into her ear. "I'd make your ass red. I'd hurt you so you never forgot it."

She comes all over me with a desperate moan. I've spent years in the field, learning to be fucking patient, but when she tightens and pulses and comes, I can't hold back. I lean in over her and fuck her like I've lost my mind. I've lost it. I fill Marjorie Dunn up. All of me pours into her. She arches underneath me, spreading her legs wider to take it all in.

And then I let myself fall onto her. Bury myself into her. I'm still inside of her, still pulsing cum into her soaked flesh, but Marjorie puts her arms around me and holds on. She strokes the back of my neck. Rubs her palms over my shoulder blades. "I liked that," she whispers, and I can hear how much she liked it in her voice. I couldn't scare her. She knew it was a fucking game all along. "Are you okay?"

It renders me speechless. What do I say to the sweet little innkeeper I just pinned down and fucked? Am I okay? Am I fucking okay?

No.

I'm lost.

Chapter Eleven

Marjorie

It's dark out in front of the house. Trees from the woods take up the grass. They're all shadows, looming above. My father stands outside in the moonlight. The breeze ruffles his hair. A crack in the woods like a branch snapping draws his attention. "It's time to go inside, sweetheart," he says.

"Are you coming?"

His hand comes down on my shoulder. There's another crack in the woods. He bends down to my level. "*Run,*" he says. "Get inside. Run."

I run as fast as I can to the front door and go inside. It locks behind me, but Dad isn't there. He was supposed to come with me. My legs don't carry me fast enough to the living room window.

"Dad." I tap my fingers on the window. "*Dad.*"

He doesn't hear me. It should be quiet enough for the sound to carry. He's not that far away. Dread squeezes my stomach. Why is he out there? The best place to be is inside. Behind the locked door. He should be in bed. Sleeping. It's late. That's what my parents always say to me. I need to get good rest so I'm ready for the morning. Being in the front yard all night is not how you get good rest.

What is there to run from?

I tap on the window again. "Dad?"

A black car pulls into the driveway. The headlights are off. That's not safe, either. They could hit him. It would be hard to see without any headlights. The front door opens, and a man climbs out. Another man comes from the backseat. Two more. The car doubles in size. My dad keeps one hand in his pocket and puts the other one out, palm facing them. He's talking to them. I can't hear what he's saying.

They get closer to him. That can't be right. My dad is a big, powerful man. Why would anyone want to surround him like that? No one needs to bother him this late. It doesn't make any sense. The car's features keep changing. One second it's boxy. The next second it's got curved lines and looks newer.

My dad's in trouble. That's what trouble looks like. It looks like being in a crowd of men in dark clothes. But why? He's never done anything to these people. He's just my dad. He stayed out too late, that's all. It's past bedtime.

"He didn't do anything wrong," I say through the window. "Stop. Dad. Come inside."

He backs up one step, but there's a man waiting behind him. When my dad turns his head, I can see that he's still speaking. His mouth moves and moves. The other men are speaking, too. They're all talking. There's no way they can hear each other. They won't be able to understand if they keep interrupting him like that.

"Listen to him," I demand, but the glass keeps my words inside with me. Anger and fear twist together in my gut. It's rude to talk over people. It's rude to ignore my dad. They can't just come here to the yard and do this. "Listen to him. Please stop talking."

One of them grabs for him.

He pulls his arm out of reach.

They swarm him like hornets. Fists fly. My dad crumples to the ground, but he stands back up. He's outnumbered. There are just too many men for him to fight off. The blows land against his body. I've never been in a fight like that. It has to hurt so much. My stomach knots up. *No, please. Not my dad. Don't hurt him like that. Don't hit him—*

A gun shines in the moonlight.

I've seen movies. I've seen my dad's gun. I've seen lots of guns in my life, and I know what it means when someone takes one out. It means that someone's going to get hurt. Badly hurt.

"Dad, come inside. Come inside right now."

I won't ask for anything else, ever again. I won't ask for toys or birthday cake or piggyback rides. I won't ask him why he's always working so much. All I need is for him to run away from those men and lock the door behind him. It's not far. He could make it.

The man with the gun steps back and points it at my dad.

"No. No. No." I raise my hand to beat at the window. Someone grabs me before I can do it. Her arms pull me back from the glass a few inches.

My mother. My mother's arms, around me. I fight against her, trying to reach the window. "Quiet," she urges. "Honey. Be quiet. I'm begging you. We need to go."

"They're hurting him."

A shout makes it through the pane of glass, and then a flash of light.

A flash like fire.

My father's body falls to the ground. None of the men move to catch him. The man with the gun stands over him, aiming it at him.

They shot my dad.

They shot him.

He's bleeding—

My mom takes advantage of my shock and pulls me through the living room. She's dragging me now, up the stairs. I can't catch my breath. I saw that gun. I saw him die. I saw him fall. The image repeats again and again and again. We go up and up. Mom wrenches open a narrow door at the end of the hall. My elbow hits the frame as we go through. She pushes me in front of her. A pounding at the door down on the first floor matches my heart. Her face gets close. "Stay quiet," she says. "Don't make a sound. Don't make any noise. Quiet."

The door closes behind her.

I'm alone.

They hurt my father.

Killed him. He's not going to get up. A low voice gets closer. Sweat gathers on the back of my neck. The attic room is shapeless. It's blowing away in the wind. It's not carpet against my palm, but sheets.

Sheets.

I'm in bed.

I push myself upright, out of the dream. I'm in a cold sweat, my heart pounding. It wasn't real. Just a dream. A horrible one, made out of a real memory. God, I hate that. I hate that the only time I see my father is in dreams about his death. I squeeze my eyes shut tighter. Another memory. I need something else to think about. The way his voice sounded, but I can't quite remember it. Tears sting at the corners of my eyes. Of course I haven't forgotten. I remember. I remember. And if I don't remember that, I remember how it felt to hold his hand when we crossed the street.

He had—he had big hands. Callused. But he never held mine too tightly.

The voice filters through the wall again.

It's getting closer. I pull the sheet over my lap and scramble toward the wall. They're here—they found me in the attic. All these years of hiding and they found me behind that same locked door. It was all for nothing if they've found me. All my mother's sacrifices. All the times I stayed quiet and didn't scream, even though I wanted to. Even though my heart was being torn from my chest.

Those men weren't familiar, though. They were strangers. And this voice sounds familiar. I swallow a cry for help and force myself to listen.

It's Sam.

It's just Sam, that's all. Sam, the mysterious guest at my inn.

I sag against the wall with relief. My heartbeat begins to settle down. It was so loud I couldn't hear anything else. Thank God it's him. Nobody else is in here with me. We're safe.

My pulse slows.

His voice gets clearer. There's a soft creak, like he's pacing the floor. People don't pace around unless they're agitated about something. There's nothing to be upset about today. We had a picnic. We went to bed together. That's all.

"No," he says.

Is he talking to himself? It doesn't sound like it. But it's the middle of the night. Too late for a phone call. I don't make a habit of eavesdropping on my guests. I can't help it this time. All's quiet in the inn, which means his voice is clear.

"Yes, I've searched."

My stomach drops. He told me that he went into the workroom out of habit. Because his work had made him into the kind of person who couldn't resist a search or a secret. Telling another person that he's done the work makes it sound like something else entirely.

It makes it sound like a job.

It sounds like a job that a CIA agent with a gun in a duffel bag and a fake ID might do.

And those kinds of jobs—

They don't end with people walking away. They end with people getting hurt. Oh, shit. Is that what he was trying to tell me before? I got caught up in how sexy he is and how much I wanted his hands on me, and I didn't listen. He told me. He said he'd hurt me. *That's what I do.* Oh, God.

I hold my breath. I can't afford to miss a single word of this conversation. Staying quiet right now might save my life the way it did all those years ago. The hairs on the back of my neck stand up. I kept myself alive for so long. This can't be how it ends.

"Listen to what I'm saying. There is no evidence. I've searched high and low. It's not here."

Chapter Twelve

Sam

"It exists. We know she has it."

I don't like the anxiety in my handler's tone. I don't like it at all. Anxiety is not an everyday part of the job. A handler never displays fear. This one especially. He's usually gruff. Demanding. And detached. This job shouldn't be any different.

Except it *is* different. Marjorie's different, for fucking sure. That shouldn't extend to the handler. He knows I'm a good operator.

It's making me suspicious. I don't like that feeling when it comes to the chain of command. Suspicion is useful in the field. You get an inkling about something, you follow it. Everyone above me should be dead sure of the job.

"I've searched every inch of this place. There's nothing."

"The intel on this was good."

"It wasn't that good or else I'd have found it already."

Because I have searched. When Marjorie was deeply asleep, I made trips to her workroom. I opened every file. I've gone through every drawer and cupboard in this place. No guest room has been left untouched. No linen closet.

"Is there a complication?" he asks flatly. All the anxiety is gone from his voice. All the emotion. He's snapped back to his usual persona. "If there is, report."

"There's no complication. It's not here."

I don't like this line of questioning. Obviously, there is a fucking complication, but he's deciding to go above my head. He's deciding to send someone else in. "This is contrary to your record."

"This is contrary to quite a few fucking things," I argue. "The intel has never been this flawed."

"The next step is to eliminate the target."

My blood runs cold, then boiling hot. "That wasn't the assignment."

"I have authorization to change the assignment parameters."

"Why the fuck—" I grit my teeth together and get a handle on my tone. If I fight with him too much, he'll assume that I've gotten emotionally involved. And maybe I have. Who the hell cares? Marjorie hasn't done a damn thing. She runs a bed and breakfast, for God's sake. Nothing she has in this building is hurting anyone. "That isn't necessary."

"If you can't locate the evidence, there are concerns about future behavior from the target."

This is the same language we've always spoken together. Hits and targets and elimination and evidence. It's all code for death and suffering. I thought I was used to it. I've had to be used to it. That's the fucking job. But I want to reach through the phone and kill him when he talks about Marjorie as a goddamn target. When he causally mentions eliminating her for some vague future behavior.

"If those concerns are based on the same intelligence that pinpointed the evidence, then it's an incorrect conclusion. I want it reviewed."

"Do you have additional data?"

Yes. That I fucking searched the Lighthouse Inn, and there is no evidence of anything involving Marjorie's father. That I have kissed her and fucked her and tasted her, and she is sweet and warm and kind. That all she's ever wanted is safe harbor. She doesn't want anything to do with the CIA or the night her father died or any of this bullshit.

"Lack of evidence. There's been no mention of any documentation."

"Subsequent review will need approval."

"This woman should be left alone." The edge of my phone bites into my palm. I'm holding the damn thing too tightly. It's cheap as hell, the way all my phones have been. They last for an assignment or two and then I get a new one. "She's an innocent."

"We have no confirmation on that."

"I'm confirming it. She's fucking innocent."

"What's the basis for your assessment?"

"I've interviewed her."

"Comprehensively?"

This heartless bastard wants to know if I've tortured her. If I've put her under physical pressure to answer me.

"A comprehensive interview wasn't in the orders. I've had numerous one-on-one conversations with her since my arrival."

A keyboard taps in the background. He's making notes for the file on Marjorie. It's a familiar enough sound, but it makes my teeth grind together.

"Your request for review has been noted."

"That's not enough. I want a guarantee that she'll be left alone until the review is complete."

"I'm not able to guarantee—"

"I want the guarantee," I insist. He's above me in the chain of command. The handler is supposed to have the final word. "She's innocent."

More tapping in the background. He's probably writing that he suspects emotional attachment. He's probably reporting that the mission has been compromised. In all my years in the service, I've never been the one to compromise anything. There have been fucked-up jobs before. Interference from the outside. I've had to call in reports like that.

"Hold your position," he says.

"Give me the time frame."

There's nothing on the other end of the line. Only silence. He hung up on me.

I almost press the button to call him back. Almost. But what the hell else would I say? I lean over the bathroom counter and stare at the call log on the phone. If I lived here with Marjorie, the screen would be filled with her name. Other people from Eben Cape. It wouldn't be a string of numbers I don't bother to memorize. They change too much and mean almost nothing. They only mean work.

There's nothing left to say to the handler. He's already written what he's going to write. Placing another call will only reinforce that he needs to take me off this job.

I put the phone down and splash water on my face instead. This is not how the job was supposed to go. It was a simple, in-and-out mission. Evidence collection. Not a fucking hit. I should have known it was fucked from the second I saw her. From the second I wanted her.

I take another thirty seconds washing my hands. If Marjorie wakes up when I get back in bed, I don't want her to suspect anything. I'll figure this out. I'm not going to let somebody come in here and take over the job.

I'm not going to let anybody hurt her.

I turn off the light and step back into the bedroom.

Rumpled sheets. Jacked-up pillows. Empty bed.

Marjorie's gone.

Chapter Thirteen

Marjorie

I don't know what to bring.

That's a problem.

I shove things into a small backpack in my bedroom, but they're just random things. Toiletries. A photo of the beach from my bedside table. My wallet. There's not enough room in the backpack for the life I've built.

That's another problem. I've made a life here. I told myself that I would always be ready to run away. I'd always be able to pick up and leave if I needed to.

Now? Now I'm swallowing guilt for not being able to take my scrapbooking supplies. I could fit some of them in the bag, but not all of them. I have two orders in progress. Two families who trusted me with their keepsakes. It pinches at my heart. I hate picturing their disappointment when I stop answering their emails and the packages never appear. It won't be the money that makes them feel the worst. It'll be losing those precious photos and clippings.

Maybe if I packed a separate bag—

No. There's no time. That would mean going down to the workroom and transferring all the items. I won't be able to return the materials at all. I wipe away tears before they can fall. I can't believe this, and at the same time, I can. I've always been afraid of this happening. I've always hoped and prayed that it wouldn't. My body trembles like this is part of the nightmare.

It feels like it.

It feels like I never went to sleep that night. I never came out of the attic. I'm still watching my father die on the same dark night. Still staying quiet. It seemed like forever until my mom came back. She'd packed light, too. A small pack with my favorite doll. A few things from her jewelry box. A couple of sets of clothes. We left everything else behind.

For this. So I could get here and buy this inn and take reservations and have a peaceful life. How did it come to this? I was so careful.

I take a deep breath and let go of my regret about the scrapbooking things. Those families will have to be happy with what they have. They'll have to be okay with having had a past at all. I don't. I have nothing from before.

"What are you doing in here?" Sam asks from the door.

I whirl around to face him and leap toward him instead. My body seems to belong to someone else. I've never hit anyone in anger, but I hurl my fists at him now. Against his shoulders and his chest. It hurts to hit him. He's strong, and all of his muscles are hard. "How dare you? How dare you? Who were you talking do? What are you going to do to me? You told me—you told me you wouldn't hurt me."

"I haven't hurt you." He puts his hands up to stop me. Sam's not fighting back. He's just blocking my punches so they don't land directly in his face.

"You're ruining everything." My voice shakes. "You knew what you were doing when you came here, and you took my whole life away. This is my whole life. I don't have anything else. Now I'm going to have to get a new one. Do you know how hard that is?"

"Yes."

I don't care. His words mean nothing to me now. He did this to me. Tears slide down my cheeks. I throw another punch, which doesn't get anywhere near him. "How dare you?"

"Marjorie, it's all right."

"No," I snap. "It's not all right. I should have known when I found you in the workroom. What were you looking for? It doesn't matter. You didn't find it, and now you're calling somebody to decide what to do about me." I meet his eyes, terror overwhelming my anger. "What are you going to do, Sam? Kill me? If you're going to do that, why don't you just do it now?"

I've been waiting all my life for this to happen. All my life, I've dreaded men showing up in the dark to do violence. That's what they always do. They come into a situation where they're not wanted and they tear it apart. It was foolish of me to think it could be different after what happened to my dad. It was foolish of me to let myself believe that Sam was safe.

He puts one hand on my cheek. "You have to trust me."

"Why would I trust you?" I aim another set of punches at his chest, but he doesn't let me get to him. He takes both of my hands in one of his and holds them close to his body. I'm still within arm's reach. I could keep trying to fight, but I don't.

"If I leave, they'll just send someone else."

"Then I'll run. Get out of my way and let me run. I'll go where they'll never find me."

"It's the CIA, Marjorie. If you run, they'll come after you."

"How do you know that? I could become anyone. I could go anywhere."

"You can't."

"I can."

"They'll send someone like me." His eyes are apologetic, and it makes me want to comfort him. That's how I got into this situation in the first place. By being a good person. By wanting to make things better for this man who is about to ruin everything. "They'll send someone worse than me. Someone who doesn't care at all about his targets."

"Oh, and you care? You just called me a target."

"I don't think of you that way, but they will." Frustration creeps into his voice.

"I still don't trust you. I'm never going to trust you." Betrayal makes my stomach hurt.

"Marjorie—" He clenches his jaw, eyes flashing. He's trying to stay calm and stoic. That's what he does. He hurts people and he's unemotional about it. But when Sam looks back into my eyes, there's something else there. He wants me to trust him. Well, he got his wish. I did trust him.

"I can't trust your word," I tell him. "I don't know anything about you. You gave me a fake name. You've searched my property. And I think maybe you slept with me—"

"No."

"Maybe you slept with me because you thought I'd tell you some secret you wanted."

"No." He grips my chin tight. "I wanted you. Sleeping with you wasn't part of the job. I could lose everything for doing that. For feeling—for feeling fucking anything at all."

"Fine. But that doesn't mean I should trust you."

"There's no one else." It's true, and it hurts. I don't have any family to defend me now. "I'm the one who's here. And I think that if you look back at the time we've spent together, you'll know you can trust me."

"What proof have you given me?"

"We played a game. And you liked it. I pretended to be an asshole. I was rough with you. You weren't afraid. You enjoyed yourself. I've never hurt you. I searched your things, yes. I could have done worse. Some of the other agents would have done much fucking worse. They would have killed you without having a discussion, Marjorie, and I didn't. I've kept my word."

"This hurts." Hot tears run wet my skin. "I hate this."

"I know. It's not going to get better. I can't take any of this back. I—" His other hand comes up to cradle my face, and Sam looks into my eyes. I've never seen sadness like this. "I don't deserve your trust. But you have to give it to me."

"Why?"

"Because I can't let anyone else hurt you, either. I have to keep you safe."

All I want is for him to hold me. It's the worst feeling. It's a sure sign that I don't know what I'm doing. I shouldn't trust anything Sam says. I shouldn't allow him to touch me. I should have gone for a weapon. A kitchen knife, maybe. That's all I have.

"Keeping me safe isn't what your job is. Clearly."

"No. It's not." Sam leans in like he wants to kiss me. I want him to kiss me. And I want him to not have done this. "My job is not to keep you safe, but I want that. I gave you my word, and I don't do that lightly. I'm not going to hurt you. I'm not going to let anybody else touch you. But I can't do that if you run away. Can you just trust me for a fucking minute so I can keep you alive? Can you trust me right now?"

I should want to tear myself out of his hands, slap him across the face, and run, but I don't.

That will only make him chase me.

Instead, I relax my body, let out a breath, and stop trying to free my hands. "Fine. I'll trust you now." I'm lying. Sam lied to me, and now I'm lying to him. I don't trust him. I don't want him. I'm searching for a way out. "Can you just give me a minute? This is a lot to take in."

Sam drops my hands. I'm disappointed when he lets go. Betrayed that he'd do it, even though I asked him to. "One minute," he says. "I need to make a plan."

He turns away and leaves. I listen to his footsteps on the stairs. My chest pounds, but I don't have time for a broken heart. Not tonight.

All I have time for is survival.

Chapter Fourteen

Sam

Marjorie wanted a minute, and I'll be damned if I don't give it to her. This place is her home. She should have a chance to say goodbye before whatever comes next. I throw on some clothes and go out to where Marjorie's car is parked out front.

This way, I'll know if she tries to leave.

Out in the brisk wind, I flip through the contacts on my phone. This kind of call is even rarer than the batshit one I had with my handler. I never thought I'd need to make it. Not on this job.

I dial the number.

Ellen picks up on the second ring. "Who's this?"

The greeting's a cover. She sounds like she's just answering a random phone call, but this is her work line. This will be the phone the agency uses to get in contact. It's risky as fuck for me to call it, but I don't have another number, and I need information. There's a serious lack of it on this run. Somebody's hiding something. Multiple people, probably. Up and down the chain of command.

"I just wanted to talk."

Ellen's a lady I've worked with before. No idea what her real name is. I've never asked, and she's never offered. Ellen is the one she goes by with me. What I know about her is that she's good at her job. She's strong and smart and ruthless. All the things I used to be. All the things that have been broken down by Marjorie Dunn.

"Can't sleep?"

Another code. She wants to know if someone else from the CIA has already shown up. "Just restless. I've been doing some thinking lately."

She might not tell me anything, even if she does know. I'm also taking the chance that she won't call my handler and report this conversation to him the second we hang up. Hell, she could already be doing it. This phone in one hand. Sending him an email with another. But I have to try. I can't have the sweet little innkeeper looking at me like I stomped on her heart. She can feel that way, but she has to be alive to feel it.

Damn it, I don't want her to feel that about me. I want her to care about me the way I care about her.

"What's on your mind?"

"Work's not going how I thought it would. I'm worried I'm going to get a bad annual review."

"Yeah—about that. Somebody from the team already asked me to take over your responsibilities for you. One of the higher-ups. I think you know him."

The handler. Yes. I fucking know him. I've never met the man in person, but I know his voice. And I know that how he sounded earlier was off. "Of course I know him. We're in regular contact."

"He wasn't himself. I guess he's got an agent who refused to fall in line. Guy couldn't pull off the latest assignment like he always does."

"Did you take the job?"

If Ellen agrees, then she's already in Eben Cape. She could be on the other side of the inn right now. I listen harder to the sounds on the line. The wind in the trees obscures everything. I lean against Marjorie's car and scan the property. There's no sign of Ellen, but that doesn't mean she's not here.

"No. I wouldn't do that to a colleague. I don't like stepping on people's toes like that."

"You've always been one of the good ones."

"So have you," she says cautiously. "You're loyal, and people know that. That's why this thing seems suspicious as all hell. Did you turn?"

"The documentation was bad," I answer, choosing every word carefully. Her question is the most dangerous one of all. If I give her the idea that I've gone rogue, she'd be within her rights to report it. She's required to report it. "I requested a review."

"Sent up some red flags."

"That's not good." There's only one silver lining, and that's Ellen's loyalty. She didn't take the job from the handler. It's enough trust for me to go on. The bad news is that he'll have somebody else on the job. Somebody less loyal to their fellow agents. Whoever the hell was willing. "Fuck."

"I came to the same conclusion. You're fucked. Whoever you are, whoever you're with, you're fucked." The identity I'm using doesn't matter to me, but Marjorie does. "You're going to have to disappear. Become somebody else."

"I don't know if that's possible."

"They have lots of resources."

I could survive on my own for a while. Walk off the job right now and blend into the shadows. Cross the border into another country. Marjorie could leave, too. If she left alone, then she'd have a chance…

But not for long. We leave the inn, and we're signing up for a lifetime of being hunted. Those are the stakes in games like these. I swore not to hurt her, and somehow it's turned into a hit on a civilian. The chain of command has already decided she's a risk, and they're concealing their reason from me. I don't know what's happening. Staying alive is going to be complicated as hell if the CIA is after us and if I'm after her at the same time.

Is that what we're looking at? Marjorie, free in the country, and me trailing after her to try to keep her safe?

"Did he say anything else to you? Make any comments?"

"No, he never has much to say. Why? Was he chatting your ear off?"

"Yes. Something's different about the job. People are getting nervous."

People like the fucking handler. People like me.

"That's the impression I got." A pause. "You don't fuck up on jobs, though. That's the part that doesn't fit."

"I don't fuck up on jobs, and he doesn't get emotional."

"I'm sorry I can't help you." Fuck. "I could call him, but—"

"No. Don't do that." That's not what I want out of Ellen. A phone call like that will put her in danger in more ways than one. "Don't draw attention to yourself."

"See? This is how I know you're loyal. You're a fucking prince in this line of work."

"You got any ideas for what's next?" It's not like me to ask another agent for help. We don't have collaborative jobs. We don't get together and trade stories. We don't tell anything to anyone. We don't talk to each other long enough to learn anything personal. Even if we did, there's nothing to learn. We don't have homes. We don't have families. I thought I could get through my career without any of that, but now I need one conversation with another person.

"Disappear." Ellen's firm. "Disappear and never look back."

"How am I supposed to do that if—"

If Marjorie has a home. That's what I don't say to Ellen. It doesn't matter if Marjorie has a home in Eben Cape. I've never had anything of the kind. I tried to find it in college. I tried at the CIA. I've done a damn good job at finding a replacement to take up my time and attention, but I always knew it would come at the cost of having any real life.

It fucking kills me to think about how hard Marjorie worked for her life. She was left with scraps, and she made the Lighthouse Inn. It's incredible. I know. Because I know everything about her. I know everything that happened to her.

It matters.

What Ellen is suggesting would be like burning the inn to the ground, and I don't want to do that.

It might be the only way to survive.

"You know any good vacation spots?"

"There's a place in Italy," Ellen offers. "Been there a couple times. Should be good for a short stay, at least. But you know. The treaties."

"Yeah." Countries work together on this kind of shit. The CIA is made up of solitary agents who have to travel across the globe. They have connections with other agencies. Countries have various diplomatic treaties. If any of those other agencies were to locate me, they'd have incentives to deport. "How are the reviews?"

"Mostly positive."

Ellen's offering me something good. A place to hide. A little piece of her own network. Connections like this are rare and secret, made up of people who never give up names, never give up locations....

Unless somebody else makes it worth it for them.

I could go to Italy with Marjorie. We'd have to fly. We'd need passports. IDs. I don't have any of that shit. Marjorie doesn't have a passport, either. She was never planning to cross any international borders. I could get new documents, but it would take time, and I'm not sure we have enough of that to spare.

"I'm thinking about a chance," I announce to Ellen. "Another line of work."

"You didn't mention that. I guess we won't be talking any time soon.

Nice of you to say your goodbyes."

"It was good working with you."

"It was good working with you, too." She laughs. We never really worked together. Solo jobs. Sometimes in the same country. Ellen's the only number I've got in my phone, besides the handler.

"It was nice to hear your voice. Hey, forget you ever heard about me, okay?"

"I don't know who this is." Ellen's voice turns brisk. "You must have had the wrong number."

The call clicks off.

I'm on my own.

Chapter Fifteen

Marjorie

Sam's on the phone again, and that's what gives me the courage to run.

Not far down the beach is a dock. The boat's not mine, but I'm friendly with the old couple who own the house. They leave the keys in a little box under the dock. I fumble for the keys and jump into the boat. The bag I tried to pack earlier was too much. I left it behind and took the black purse that's been my go-bag since I turned eighteen.

My real go-bag. Not the one I tried to shove my life into back in my bedroom. I don't know what I was thinking. Clothes? Keepsakes? No one needs those things to stay alive. You need a bit of cash and an ID. Everything else can be replaced. Even the ID, if you try hard enough.

God, it's exhausting. Being on the run. Hiding. Trying to build a life that's real enough to keep a roof over your head and fake enough that you never get caught.

I used to have a bigger bag packed up, just in case. Eben Cape made me lax. Lax enough to trust a hitman. And now I'm paying the price.

Walking away from everything—that's the price. It feels heavy. My stomach churns at the thought of the empty inn and the unreturned scrapbooks and the friends I've made. Emily will be worried. There's a good chance I'll never be able to tell her that I'm okay. I'll never talk to her again. If I can make it to tomorrow in one piece, I'll never see Eben Cape again.

I start the motor, untie the boat, and haul the ropes in with me. It's so damn loud. My only hope is that Sam doesn't realize I've gone. He was on the other side of the inn, not facing the water. If he hears this—

It'll be too late. He's a strong man, but he can't run as fast as a speedboat.

I steer myself away from the shore. Cold water stings my cheeks. I miss Sam. I miss the heat of the fire he made for me. I miss the safety of his body.

The fake safety of his body. That was never real. He was never here to keep me safe. He was only here to invade my life and find evidence.

I've had nightmares for years. They always involved the men who killed my father coming to find me. In my dreams, their faces were never clear. I knew them by their dark clothes and their rough hands. I never imagined it would be Sam. But then—I recognized him, didn't I? I knew when he walked in the front door of the inn that he'd be a danger to me. What I didn't expect is that he would make me feel so good. That having him with me would bring me back to life.

It's humiliating. It was easy for him to get under my skin. I've been so starved for contact with a man that I fell for his lies. I can't shake the feeling that there was some truth there, too. That's what makes it so painful. He meant what he said. Which things, though? It's impossible to say. Maybe he was lying about hating his job. Maybe he didn't actually want to eat a BLT. Nothing is out of the question.

His body didn't lie. He couldn't fake that. It's so wrong to remember it. So wrong to keep finding ways that he told the truth. But I felt it when we were together in bed. I felt his need and his hunger and his relief. That couldn't have been a lie.

What does it mean?

Anything?

My heart twists. I just don't want to believe it was all for nothing, even if that's what all the evidence says. What I felt wasn't nothing. What he felt wasn't nothing.

Thinking about him isn't going to help me now, though. My emotions have to be second to staying alive. I need to concentrate on the water. The moon is out, but otherwise it's dark. Much too late to be boating. It feels too late to be running for my life. This should have happened earlier. I resent that it took so long. I had so much time to build the inn and make friends and get comfortable. If the CIA wanted me, they should have killed me before I did all of that.

Another motor hums over the water. I push my hair out of my face and turn my head, keeping one hand on the wheel.

It's back behind me. Not very far. A man dressed in black is driving it. I can't see much of him, but for a second I think it's Sam. My heart skips a beat. That's how Sam looked when he first showed up at the inn. He looked dangerous. A little rough. If he came for me, then maybe I'll stop running. It would be better to be on the run with someone else. I don't want to be alone.

I'm so tired of being alone. So tired of everyone leaving at the end of the weekend. My hand moves on the wheel, turning it just a little so I can get a clearer view of the other boat while I skim the water.

A gust of wind catches in the man's hood and blows it back from his face.

It's not Sam.

My stomach drops. That man is definitely not him, and he's definitely after me. There's no one out here tonight.

Oh, God. Sam was right. They sent someone else. Someone worse.

I could scream with frustration. I didn't do anything to these people. I didn't do anything wrong at all. I was a child, and someone murdered my father. My mother hid me in the attic. I stayed alive. Is that such a crime that I should be hunted down? Over what? I don't have any evidence. I don't have what they're looking for.

I have nothing. I'm back to nothing. I'm back in that attic again, holding my breath to stop myself from crying and waiting for my mom to come back.

She's never coming back. I've lost everything. No matter what I do, I keep losing everything. Heat spreads across my face. Why did I even bother?

Sam's never coming back. I'm never going to return to my life. It's over. I might as well be dead. Grief surges up in a cold splash. I worked for this, damn it. I worked and worked and worked, and it was all pointless.

Black water ripples below my boat. Should I do it? Should I dive in and disappear under the surface? It might get this over with. If I jumped in now, there's a chance I could get to shore and run. Or the man driving the boat could catch up with me and steal me out of the water. Getting wet and cold is a guarantee I won't make it far. I'm not in that kind of shape.

No. I'm not going to abandon the boat. I'm going to get away from whoever is chasing me. My mother would never want me to give up. I won't throw away everything she did for me. I'll fight to the bitter end for her.

For me, too. I might be the only one who knows, but I'm not going to give up on myself.

I veer away, cutting too close to the shore. The motor skims across the shallows, and I cut out again, just far enough to keep from losing the blades. My heartbeat skyrockets. The last thing I need is to run the boat aground in the middle of a grand escape.

I'm going back to the cove.

We had a picnic there, and it's not going to feel good to relive those memories. It's not going to feel good to know that Sam was lying to me the whole time. That the peace we shared together was a lie.

But it's my best chance at staying alive. It makes sense. If you're alive, you can feel pain. You can feel heartbreak. I certainly do.

The rocks from the cove extend out into the water. The locals in Eben Cape know about it, but at least once a summer, a tourist who doesn't know better has an accident and ruins a boat. The cove itself is secluded, and the rocks are even sharper. The cave there isn't deep, but it doesn't look shallow from the water.

I could hide until he's gone.

I ignore the instinct that says this man won't give up just because I hide in a cave. That the CIA might never leave me alone, no matter how angry or innocent I am. This is only about staying alive for the next fifteen minutes.

After that, I'll focus on the next fifteen.

And no matter what, I won't think of Sam again.

Chapter Sixteen

Sam

The motor starts up a second after the call disconnects.

A boat motor.

Fuck.

I sprint around the inn and down to the beach. The boat's already pulling out from a dock a short distance down the shore. Marjorie's driving it. Her dark hair whips in the wind. She aims it out into the ocean, but as soon as she's got some breathing room, she cuts left.

A shout almost gets away from me. I want to yell her name. Bring her back. But I don't want to give her away. If someone's watching from the road, yelling for her would be the biggest mistake I could make.

I keep my damn mouth shut.

It doesn't matter. Another motor fires from farther down the shore. The sound makes my heart race. I try to think of it as data. It's just a fucking sound. A boat motor. Could mean anything in a seaside town like Eben Cape. I can't see anything yet. I need confirmation before I lose my shit.

The hum gets louder and louder, and it pops into view around a curve on the shore.

This is no tourist. This is no lobsterman from Eben Cape. This is an agent. He's all in black, and he doesn't so much as glance in my direction as he speeds by. Marjorie doesn't have much of a head start.

My first instinct is to swim after her, but it's the wrong one. I can't swim faster than a fucking speedboat. The water will only slow me down.

Marjorie went left.

Deliberately.

That's the direction we went to that cove down the beach. How long did we walk? Fifteen minutes? Couldn't have been much more than a mile. I don't need fifteen minutes to run it. She just has to keep herself alive until I get there.

With no weapons. With nothing. I know Marjorie doesn't have a gun. I turned the inn upside down, and I never saw one.

I pat my holster. I have my gun. That's the only break I'm going to get.

Waves reach for my ankles while I sprint down the beach. The boats are still out there. Their size gets harder to judge when I'm running. How far was that goddamn cove? I'd give anything for a boat right now, but I don't pass a single one I could steal. Not even a rowboat. I haven't run this fast in years. My jobs these days mostly involve infiltration. Dark basements in foreign countries. They don't involve beachside sprints. But if I get there too late, I'll never forgive myself.

The rocky crag of the cove rises up out of the beach ahead of me. I put on another burst of speed. Marjorie's boat rocks out in the water.

Where the hell is she?

Not steering it. She could be inside. Shot. Dead.

Movement on the sand catches my eye. The sweet little innkeeper scrambles out of the water. I have her in sight, but the other boat—

He's up ahead. Turning around. I still have time.

Marjorie lifts her head and startles when she sees me. I must look exactly like him. Even running full-tilt across the beach, I still catch the moment when she recognizes me. Her eyes fly open wide, and she holds one arm out.

She reaches for me.

I pull her close for a brief, tight hug. It's not enough. Not even fucking close. She bought herself enough time to get to shore and be in my arms before that bastard comes back. He's maneuvering the boat over submerged rocks. Any second now, he'll jump out and come through the shallows.

Letting go of her is the last thing I want, but I do it. I take her chin in my hand and look into her eyes. "Run."

She sucks in a breath at the word. It freezes her in place.

"Run," I say again and give her a push. The beach isn't safe. The sand isn't fucking safe. Not even the cove. I don't want her pinned against the rocks. I want her free, even if I never see her again.

She runs.

Finally.

A splash from the water draws my attention. I draw my weapon as I turn toward it. The first bullet skims by my head. He's determined, then. He's going to end both of us. Firing while he's still in the fucking water. I hate the sight of him.

Because he's me.

He's the man I became over the years at the CIA. I'm the figure stalking through the water and firing bullets through people's lives. I'm the one who dropped in out of nowhere, shredded things to pieces, and disappeared before morning. Who could ever love a sick bastard like that? Who would ever waste a life on him? The man who's coming at me through the water isn't worth a picnic, much less the heart of a woman like Marjorie Dunn.

He fires again, and I get my first shot off. It goes into the waves.

I need motion. The cove is convenient enough. The rock-studded sand makes my movements more unpredictable, and I can get above him, if I can avoid a bullet through the head. One strikes the rock next to me. I jump into that space and find enough cover to wedge my shoulder behind.

Another shot.

He lets out a furious growl. It's a display of emotion I would never expect from an agent. What the fuck is going on here? Is my handler the one who turned? Did somebody get to him? Because CIA agents engaged in lethal missions don't lose their shit about missing the first few shots. They keep firing until the goal is accomplished.

His gun comes back up, and now the bullets come fast. Wild. He's not a very good shot. Who is this motherfucker? An actual agent? He should be better than this, unless he's injured in some way that's not obvious.

Or unless he's not actually an agent.

It wouldn't be the first time I've encountered an outside hire. Plenty of organizations outsource. They'll pay cash to have the dirtiest jobs cleaned up. What matters is timeliness and efficiency.

One bullet comes too close for comfort, and I try to get more of my body behind the rock. I take a deep breath. Steady myself. My next bullet comes close but doesn't hit him. It does put him off-balance. He takes a split second to reload, and more bullets fly into the rock around me.

I feel the same urge. I want to empty all of my bullets into him. I'll do anything to stop him from hurting Marjorie, including gratuitous violence.

But I don't.

I wait.

I think of the sweet, kind innkeeper running across the sand. Part of saving her is buying time.

I've never been more grateful for this fucking job. The one that emptied me of all my hope for a better life and shaped me into a heartless killer. My hands are steady under the hail of bullets. My heart beats normally. I don't flinch away from the impact of metal on rock.

He needs to be about ten feet closer.

The agent's movements are rough. Unpracticed. It makes me wonder if he's been sidelined. It's clear he hasn't been in the field recently because a seasoned field agent would have put a bullet in my head on the first shot. There would have been no second. I focus in on him. I'm a seasoned field agent. I won't need many chances.

I just need the best one.

I count to five, then count again. It should be enough. If this shot goes wild, if I miss and the adrenaline surge gives him enough power to chase her, she'll have a good head start.

He's still shooting.

I aim for his chest, let out a breath, and pull the trigger.

It hits. I keep my weapon raised in case he's wearing body armor.

He's not. The bullet drops him to the rocks and the water. His gun sinks under a wave. When he doesn't reach for it, I abandon my cover and go to him.

"Motherfucker," he says, the end of the word drowning in a gurgle of blood.

I know that voice.

It's my handler. I never knew his name. I never saw his face. I'd know that voice anywhere. I crouch down next to him. He won't be alive much longer. "Why?"

A ghostly smile tugs at his lips. "Wanted to finish the job."

"What job?"

"Killed her dad." His breathing is labored. I don't think he feels the rocks underneath him or the water soaking into his clothes. "Wife ran with the kid. Only thing. I never finished."

The light goes out of his eyes. He came here to complete the one job he never finished. No wonder he's a stickler for getting things done. He couldn't do it himself, and now he never will.

Chapter Seventeen

Marjorie

The first helicopter appears in the sky at the same time Sam stands up from the body.

He shot that man dead. My heart went wild when all those bullets were flying. I thought they'd both die. I thought I would watch another man I love die the same way as my father. I press myself harder against the cove, but Sam comes toward me with a calm, sure expression on his face. He beckons to me. *Come here.*

I go to him. After all the gunfire, I need safety. I need it from him. As soon as I'm in reach, he folds his arms around me and holds me close. He's warm in the night chill, and I bury my face in his chest. Another helicopter swoops into view overhead. Two more come after. Bright lights shine down on the beach. On the man's body.

"I need you to listen to me," he murmurs into my ear, his breath warm on my skin. "The people in the helicopters aren't going to hurt us."

"How do you know?"

He shakes his head. "Something was off about the mission. The man I killed—he was my handler. It wasn't official."

"The CIA didn't send you here?"

"Someone higher up might have wanted to know if you had information, but it was personal for him."

My body trembles harder. Sam runs his palms over my back. "Personal how?"

"It's over, Marjorie. Nobody else is going to be looking for you."

He sounds so confident, but how could Sam know? "Are you sure?"

Sam nudges me until I tip my face up to look into his eyes. "That was the man who killed your father. You and your mother were supposed to die along with him, but you escaped. It's dogged him for the rest of his career. He wanted to finish the job."

"There were other men." Panic rises. "They could be looking—"

"No. If there were other agents, this would have happened a long time ago. The rest of them have moved on or retired or been killed. It's done. You can go back to your life."

The first helicopter lands on the grass in someone's back yard. This is going to be news in Eben Cape. A swarm of CIA helicopters invading? Oh, God. The gossip. The rumors. Black uniforms pour out of the helicopter. It makes my head spin and my throat tight. "I don't like this. What's going to happen?"

"Nothing. Marjorie. Look at me." I look into Sam's dark eyes. "They're not going to touch you. I'll make sure of it. Okay?"

The first agents arrive, running along the beach toward us. "Rogue agent," the first one says. "Status report?"

"He's dead. Body's over that way."

"Any injuries?"

"No."

A second agent jogs up next to him. "We'll need her for questioning. Bring her this way."

Sam puts his body between me and the agents. "Anything you want to ask her, you can do it here."

More men gather around us. They all have questions. Rapid-fire ones. I don't know how they process any of my answers. How long have I lived in Eben Cape? Has any other man like that agent ever checked into the Lighthouse Inn? Do I have any documents relating to my father's history? Have I been in contact with anyone claiming to be a CIA agent?

I answer the best I can, but my voice doesn't want to work. I'm afraid to say the wrong thing.

"We'll need you to come with us, ma'am," the man in front says.

"Leave her the fuck alone," Sam snaps. "This whole goddamn mess is a consequence of a rogue agent. You did this to her. And now you're going to be civilized and let her go back to her life."

"Sir, your involvement in the mission—"

"The agency is going to show her some fucking courtesy." Sam's voice gets deadly sharp. "Or I'll go on the evening news and tell the world how badly you've fucked up."

The other man's eyes go wide at the suggestion that Sam would expose them. It's against their rules, I'm sure. And it has to be dangerous for Sam. The CIA could come after him for doing it. How would he ever feel safe again?

Maybe he's never felt safe in his life.

The agents exchange glances. A man who would make that threat is someone to be reckoned with, I suppose. An uncertain energy hangs in the air. It seems like Sam was right. The man who came after me was working on his own orders. It would be a scandal for the CIA to have lost control of someone so completely that they came to Eben Cape and gunned down a woman on the beach.

Me. If they gunned *me* down on the beach. Another tremor rocks my body, and Sam runs a soothing hand over the small of my back. I was so close to dying tonight. I'm only alive because of Sam.

"Debriefing's not optional," the other agent says, looking Sam in the eye. The beach is swarmed with agents and helicopter shells. The rotors beating in the wind were the loudest sounds I've ever heard. They're still echoing in my brain.

"Understood. Can you give us a fucking minute?"

Yes, apparently, they can. The men step away, leaving Sam and me in a small pocket of peace on the sand. He's blocking my view of the dead man with his own body. All I can see is a team of people gathered around the rocks near the cove, anyway. All I want to see is Sam.

I lean into him and put my arms around his waist. Under the noise of the waves and the agents, I can hear his heartbeat. Sam holds me until I catch my breath.

It takes a long time. I almost lost my life tonight. The shocking part is how sad it made me to walk away from everything. From my business and my friends and the little home I've made for myself. But it made me saddest to be leaving Sam. That doesn't make a lot of sense, I know. I only met him a few days ago. Even now, in his arms, the thought of being separated from him forever hurts my heart. I want him with me on a level that's much deeper than a reservation at the inn or even a marriage license. It's his body I need close to mine. His heartbeat. The scent of his skin.

It wasn't enough time. Not by far. I want to know everything about the man who came to my door looking for peace and found me instead. I could have been peace—for a little while. The picnic was peaceful.

Though it wasn't me, after all. It was his handler. His job. That was the source of his pain.

I'm not calm enough to figure it all out. Not tonight.

"What do we do next?"

Sam pauses at my question. His hands spread out on my back. We're as close as we can be without being naked and in bed together. "You're going to go back to the inn. You can have your life back, Marjorie."

My life. The Lighthouse Inn. Phone calls with Emily. A trip to the antique shop. Visitors around the holidays, then a winter lull. Scrapbooking. I'll be able to finish those projects and return them to the families.

That's my life, but it was different with Sam in it. More exciting. More intriguing. My body felt awake for the first time in years. If I'm going to go back to my life, then he should come with me.

"What about you?"

A brief, sad silence answers all of my questions before he speaks. I wish he wouldn't say it. I wish he wouldn't. We could let the waves answer for us. I have a silly hope that we could walk away together right now. Disappear into the shadows. But no—that wouldn't work. This whole incident is proof of that. Someone always comes along and finds you if you're trying to hide.

"I'll have to go with them," Sam admits. I hug him tighter, as if a hug could keep him in Eben Cape with me instead of watching him disappear into one of those helicopters. "They have questions. It will take some time to give them answers."

Because, of course, if his handler was a rogue agent, then Sam could be one, too. I don't know much about government agencies, but I do know that anyone who was involved with the handler will have to talk about what happened.

"How much time?"

He huffs out a breath as if this question is the one that has finally gotten the better of him. "I don't know."

It could be weeks. It could be years. It could be forever. It feels like goodbye, and that hurts more than the cold or the fear. Goodbye always hurts the most.

Chapter Eighteen

Sam, one month later

The one positive to the situation is that I don't have to worry about finding a place to stay. The CIA puts me up in a room in what could be a well-maintained hotel from the 1990s. It's not a hotel. It's a CIA property for agents who have been involved in something fucked-up, which I have.

Until this year, I wouldn't have cared. Now, after Marjorie, the beige paint on the walls tests my patience after three days. I have to use all my training to keep myself from losing my shit. I never do. Not in front of my interviewers, anyway. Some late nights I pace back and forth along the industrial carpet and try to remember every goddamn detail of the Lighthouse Inn. Every thoughtful decoration Marjorie found at one antique shop or another. The light through the window in my guest room.

Marjorie in my bed. Marjorie in my arms. Marjorie sighing as her lips met mine.

I've been captured as an undercover agent in enemy territory before. This is a special kind of torture.

They follow the usual procedure when it comes to the debriefing. Every possible question is put to me every possible way over the course of the full month. Different interviewers take different stances across the table from me. Some of them act like longtime friends. Some of them want to play the bad cop.

All of them get the same answers.

The mission came down from my handler.

He did a bunch of suspicious shit.

I never had instructions from anyone else.

There was no evidence at the inn.

The final interviewer isn't an interviewer at all. He's three steps up in the chain of command, and he flips through my file while he sits across from me. It's half an inch thick. Opaque records of the work I've done for the CIA. Commendations and code-word summaries, one after the other. None of those papers comes close to Marjorie's bed and breakfast. "Anything else you wanted to disclose?"

"Before you fire me, you mean."

He closes the file and looks at me over his glasses. "Several of your answers suggested that the mission was compromised."

"It wasn't my mission in the first place."

"There was an entanglement."

Yes, there fucking was. My heart has been entangled with the pretty little innkeeper since the first moment I saw her. The feelings didn't fade over the course of the debriefing. If anything, they've gotten stronger. Marjorie sleeps next to me in my dreams. I can't stop replaying my memories of the time we spent together. It was hardly any time at all. One of my shortest missions. But it changed everything. She showed me what I needed, years after I stamped out any hope of that.

It's over for me. The job. Even if he doesn't fire me, I'll never be able to go another minute without thinking of her. She'll always be in the back of my mind. That's why agents aren't supposed to have families. It takes away your ability to think rationally. Love overpowers everything else.

"If you want to stay on the force, there can be no further contact."

I can keep my job if I stay away from Marjorie Dunn. They'll make it simple. I'll be overseas, on missions that force me to be out of contact for weeks at a time. They'll keep me running down the more dangerous foreign actors and put me in increasingly difficult situations.

I'll never see her again.

Going back to Eben Cape means leaving my life behind. Everything I've worked for over the years. Everything I've done. It's nothing in the outside world. No one can ever know the details. I'll have to start over from scratch.

Bullshit. I wouldn't. Not if Marjorie would have me.

"I'm done."

That's how it ends. Decades in the CIA. Countless hours on the edge of death. A trail of dead bodies all across the planet. My entire career.

Over.

I turn in my gun and my badge. There's nothing else to give. I wait an hour for a go-between at the CIA to supply me with the first ID in years that has my real name. I sign a hundred sheets of paper. Multiple transfers are made into my bank accounts. And then the man who gave my final interview drives me to a used-car lot on the edge of town.

I buy the first decent-looking vehicle in cash, get behind the wheel, and drive toward Eben Cape. It's enough of a distance that I have time to come to terms with what I've just done. There's a chance Marjorie won't want anything to do with me.

As the miles disappear behind me, so does my fear. The chance of the pretty little innkeeper turning me away is almost nothing. And if she does, I'll survive. I've spent my life learning how to do it. All that matters is that she's safe and happy.

It's late afternoon when I pull up in front of the Lighthouse Inn. Almost sunset. The door opens as easily as it did the first day I met Marjorie Dunn.

Just like that day, she's behind the scarred oak desk.

Just like that day, my heart stops at the sight of her.

She's hopeful and beautiful, and I'm in love with her. Every part of her. The way her eyes light up when I enter the room. The way her cheeks flush. The way tears glisten in her eyes.

I approach the desk. "I'd like a room, if you have one available."

"Of course. Any one you'd like." Her chin quivers as she takes out the ledger and pushes it across the countertop toward me.

I take the pen in my hand and write my real name.

Sam Brewer

"Are you here for business or pleasure?"

I'm here for my life. That's what I'm here for. "Pleasure."

"How long will you stay?" Marjorie's voice trembles.

"Forever," I tell her. "If you'll let me."

Marjorie scrambles up onto the desk, climbs over her ledger, and throws herself into my arms.

Chapter Nineteen

Marjorie, six months later

A toddler in a high-chair laughs, the whole inn lighting up with the sound. It's a baby belly laugh and it might as well be the soundtrack of the whole summer. That joyful laugh, along with so many other voices. A newlywed couple teases each other on the way out to the beach, bathing suits on and towels slung over their shoulders. The toddler's mother leans in with a damp cloth to wipe the little one's cheeks. It's loud and chaotic and everything breakfast should be on a day like today.

I got their food out just in time. It's all on the table now. The day has officially begun.

They're happy.

I slip away into my workroom. When we have a full house like this, I have to get up just before sunrise to have all the food finished on time. It's a real accomplishment. It counts for something, putting a meal on the table. It counts for these people especially. Even if they never stay at the Lighthouse Inn again, they'll have the memory to take with them. No one had to worry about breakfast when they got up. It had already been prepared and set out.

It feels good to see the happiness on their faces.

It feels good to feel my own happiness.

I sit down at the worktable and open the cover of my latest project.

This scrapbook isn't from a family on Etsy.

This one is for me.

The day after Sam came back, he drove me to a little camera shop in Eben Cape and spent an hour asking the owner a thousand questions about cameras and lenses and memory cards. We walked out that day with a camera that might as well be a spaceship. It's one of our projects together. He's better at photography than I am, but I'll give him a run for his money. I took a picture of him last month standing in the water in a patch of orange from the sunset that takes my breath away.

It's already in the scrapbook, alongside a block of my own handwriting. I don't always include the date the photo was taken, but I did for that one. We'd stolen away from the inn after dinner and come to the shore.

The best part was afterward, when we walked back home. No need to run. Not anymore. Sneaking away is an act of pleasure because we have the Lighthouse Inn to come back to. We have each other.

Today's page is about a trip we took to the antique store. Emily and Mateo went with us. Maybe antiquing isn't the most exciting double date, but I've never been happier to watch my friends poke through aisles of treasure. After a while, I found Sam in a secluded corner by himself.

"Look," he said as I came close, sliding a hand over his shoulder. I'll take any excuse to touch him after that month he was away. Sam turned toward me, opening his palms to show me something small and polished.

A Christmas ornament.

"It reminds me of the inn," he said. "Someone else must have loved bed and breakfasts, too."

"You'll have to wait quite a while to hang it on the tree," I pointed out. Months and months. It was a long time until Christmas.

"Good. I want to spend every minute between now and then in your bed."

"I love you," I told him. It still felt new.

"I love you," he said.

Is it embarrassing to lock your legs around a man's waist in an antique shop? I suppose it could be, but I don't care. That's what I did.

I've chosen four photos from that day. One I took with the self-timer on the camera. All four of us outside the shop. One Sam took of me during lunch afterward. One I took of him from the next aisle over, his head bowed over a shelf of old books. And one of the two of us walking on the sidewalk, my hand slung around his back and his arm over my shoulder. That's my favorite one. It's tangible evidence that we were there together.

I lay them out on the page and write down the story of that day. We went to the antique shop with our friends. We had lunch. We came home.

It's both simple and priceless. The kind of thing I wish I had for all my favorite memories. We're making up for lost time with this book.

It doesn't take long to create the page. I've had it laid out in my head since we got home from the antique store and Sam put the Christmas ornament on the dresser in our bedroom.

When I'm done, I close the book and go to find him.

He's out in the yard chopping wood, the summer sun beating down on his golden skin and hard muscles. He's the opposite of the man who walked into the inn months ago. He was dark then. Haunted. Now he's light.

Sam swings the axe one more time, embedding it into the stump he uses to split the wood. He stalks toward me, a heart-skipping grin on his face, and pushes me into the side of the inn. He kisses as hard as he split that wood. Passionate. Sharp.

"What are you doing out here? Were you getting ready to run?"

"No." I can't get enough of him. I want him with me always. I push myself into him. He's hard and strong, but he's not dangerous. Not to me. "I just came to find you."

"How long are you going to do that for?"

"How long will you let me?"

His hand runs down over my waist. My hip. "'Til the end of time, Marjorie. You come looking, and I'll be here."

"Chopping wood?" I kiss him back. It's hard to stop. I'll have things to do around the inn soon enough. There's a whole summer day to get back to. A whole summer night. "Even in the winter?"

"Hell, no. I want to be between your thighs. Here, where it's warm."

He nudges my thighs apart with his knee. "Sam. We're outside. Anyone could see us."

"I don't care." He pulls me closer and bends down to kiss the side of my neck. "I want you. You're beautiful out here."

"So are you." Sweat shines on his skin from swinging the axe. He's always hot, though. I'm always on fire from looking at him. From touching him. It's never going to end. "But we can't."

"But you feel so goddamn good." He pushes me down onto his leg. It's so filthy it makes me gasp. "You taste as good as you feel. Even better."

"How do I taste?" I'm going to let him take me upstairs. That's what I'll do. I'll be quiet. I won't cause a scene with the guests.

"Sweet," he murmurs into my ear. "Like home."

Epilogue

Sam

I'm patient for my pretty little innkeeper.

She spends her days making all the guests so damn happy that they scramble for bookings next year. It's like that every weekend. They all want their time at the Lighthouse Inn. They all want to come back to her.

So do I.

It doesn't matter if we're apart for twenty minutes. I miss her like I've been gone for months on the other side of the world.

This twenty minutes is worth it.

Marjorie's already in bed. I make one more tour of the Lighthouse Inn, locking up for the night. I installed better locks than the ones she had when I came back home. The real security is lying in bed next to her every night.

It's calm in the inn when I finish my round. Quiet. Ocean waves roll on the shore outside. Parents always marvel at how fast their kids fall asleep at the inn. The ocean is the best white noise machine. It'll cover up the sounds Marjorie's about to make for me.

I wait another five minutes. I want to catch her when she's just starting to relax. Her mind wanders at the end of the day. Some people like to read a book before bed, but Marjorie likes to look out the window and plan out future pages in her scrapbook.

There won't be any photos of the next hour we spend together. They'll exist in my mind.

Two more minutes.

I let my anticipation build. I used to wait hours in the dark. In the rain. In the cold. Wounded. Tortured. Survival was the only reward, and then what did I get? Another job. More pain. More emptiness.

Now my life is so full of Marjorie that I'm surprised the roof of the inn stays on. I'm glad it does. She loves this place, and her work here, and her guests.

She loves me. Her first-ever scrapbook is going to be filled with photos of me, which is something else I never knew I needed. My entire career was about never being witnessed. Never being photographed. Staying in the dark. Disappearing without a trace. I want her to see me and to know me.

It's a miracle she does. I know that. A miracle she saw through the shell I built up over my years in the service. I don't have to be that asshole with her.

Well, sometimes I do. But she likes it.

I climb the stairs, keeping my footsteps light so none of them creak. She'll know I'm coming. I never let her fall asleep completely without reassurance that I'm beside her. But silence adds to the surprise.

The bedroom door is half-open. Our bedroom door. It's the first permanent place to sleep I've had since I signed my contract with the CIA. I know how it sounds. Being impressed with a bedroom is weird as hell, but it's the small things that make a difference. My own bed. My own pillow. My own things, kept in the bedside table.

A wallet with my ID inside. Next to that, I keep a photo of Marjorie on the beach in a little red bathing suit. She's standing in the shallow water, a big smile on her face. It's the best picture I've ever seen of anyone. My favorite. I just love the look of her in the sunshine. Carefree and happy, the way she was meant to be.

I slip inside.

Marjorie's in bed, her face turned toward the window, her dark hair spread out on the pillow. Her eyes are closed. I've timed this perfectly. She'll have had time to think about her scrapbook pages, and her thoughts have wandered away while she waits for me.

I make no sound as I cross the room.

No sound as I put my hand over her mouth and climb onto the bed beside her. One motion.

Her eyes snap open and meet mine. I've never seen more beautiful eyes than Marjorie Dunn's. I've never seen them look more beautiful than they do right now. Her breathing picks up. The sheet over her chest rises and falls in a quick, surprised rhythm.

"Don't make a sound."

She nods her head, agreeing.

"The lock on your front door was flimsy as hell, sweetheart. Any man could walk right in. Unfortunately for you, it was me. There's nothing you can do to stop this, understand?"

Marjorie nods again. She was relaxed before, on her way to dreamland, but now her fearful, hot energy fills the room. The pretty little innkeeper loves these games. I never warn her ahead of time. That's how she likes it best. Most nights, I lull her into a false sense of security with kisses and promises.

And then, on nights like tonight…

I bend low to speak into her ear. "If you please me, maybe I'll let you go."

Her eyes plead with me for more. Marjorie's nod is almost frantic. Her lips press against my palm. Kissing me when I'm pretending to be a bastard makes my heart clench.

"You'd be good at it. You're goddamn beautiful. And I bet if I spread you open and tasted you, it would be like heaven. If you can let me take what I want without making a fucking sound…"

I look into her eyes. She's impatient already. This is how she's always been with me. Desperate for everything I can give her.

No one has ever wanted me so much. I don't know why I ever thought I could get this feeling from dirty jobs in the CIA. The only person who could offer it is in the bed with me now. Marjorie squirms under the sheet. She'll be wet for me already. Goddamn, it's good. I can count on her. I can count on home.

I'm not alone anymore. Not out there with a gun and a fake ID. I'm where I belong.

"Maybe I'll let you go." Marjorie whimpers under my hand. "Or maybe I'll keep you forever."

* * * *

Also from 1001 Dark Nights and Skye Warren, discover Finale and The Bishop.

Sign up for the 1001 Dark Nights Newsletter
and be entered to win a Tiffany Key necklace.

There's a contest every month!

Go to www.1001DarkNights.com to subscribe.

**As a bonus, all subscribers can download
FIVE FREE exclusive books!**

Discover 1001 Dark Nights Collection Nine

DRAGON UNBOUND by Donna Grant
A Dragon Kings Novella

NOTHING BUT INK by Carrie Ann Ryan
A Montgomery Ink: Fort Collins Novella

THE MASTERMIND by Dylan Allen
A Rivers Wilde Novella

JUST ONE WISH by Carly Phillips
A Kingston Family Novella

BEHIND CLOSED DOORS by Skye Warren
A Rochester Novella

GOSSAMER IN THE DARKNESS by Kristen Ashley
A Fantasyland Novella

THE CLOSE-UP by Kennedy Ryan
A Hollywood Renaissance Novella

DELIGHTED by Lexi Blake
A Masters and Mercenaries Novella

THE GRAVESIDE BAR AND GRILL by Darynda Jones
A Charley Davidson Novella

THE ANTI-FAN AND THE IDOL by Rachel Van Dyken
A My Summer In Seoul Novella

A VAMPIRE'S KISS by Rebecca Zanetti
A Dark Protectors/Rebels Novella

CHARMED BY YOU by J. Kenner
A Stark Security Novella

HIDE AND SEEK by Laura Kaye
A Blasphemy Novella

DESCEND TO DARKNESS by Heather Graham
A Krewe of Hunters Novella

BOND OF PASSION by Larissa Ione
A Demonica Novella

JUST WHAT I NEEDED by Kylie Scott
A Stage Dive Novella

THE SCRAMBLE by Kristen Proby
A Single in Seattle Novella

Also from Blue Box Press

THE BAIT by C.W. Gortner and M.J. Rose

THE FASHION ORPHANS by Randy Susan Meyers and M.J. Rose

TAKING THE LEAP by Kristen Ashley
A River Rain Novel

SAPPHIRE SUNSET by Christopher Rice writing as C. Travis Rice
A Sapphire Cove Novel

THE WAR OF TWO QUEENS by Jennifer L. Armentrout
A Blood and Ash Novel

THE MURDERS AT FLEAT HOUSE by Lucinda Riley

THE HEIST by C.W. Gortner and M.J. Rose

SAPPHIRE SPRING by Christopher Rice writing as C. Travis Rice
A Sapphire Cove Novel

MAKING THE MATCH by Kristen Ashley
A River Rain Novel

Discover More Skye Warren

The Bishop
A Tanglewood Novella

A million dollar chess piece goes missing hours before the auction.

Anders Sorenson will do anything to get it back. His family name and fortune rests on finding two inches of medieval ivory. Instead he finds an injured woman with terrible secrets.

He isn't letting her go until she helps him find the piece. But there's more at stake in this strategic game of lust and danger. When she confesses everything, he might lose more than his future. He might lose his heart.

* * * *

Finale
A North Security Novella

Francisco Castille, the exiled Duke of Linares, knows his duty. Even in modern times, the line must continue. So he'll marry and produce an heir.

Yes, a wife will fit into his well-ordered life.

Instead he ends up with the brilliant pianist Isabella. Strong. Spirited. And highly disobedient. She rebels against every custom and every rule, threatening his careful balance.

Francisco never backs away from a challenge.

Isabella never bows down to anyone.

This scorching hot battle of wills may leave both of them broken.

Private Property
Rochester Trilogy Book 1
By Skye Warren
Now available.

When I signed up for the nanny agency, I didn't expect a remote mansion on a windswept cliff. Or a brooding billionaire who resents his new role.

His brother's death means he's now in charge of a moody seven year old girl. She's lashing out at the world, but I can handle her. I have to. I need the money to finish my college degree. As long as I can avoid the boss who alternately mocks me and coaxes me to reveal my darkest secrets.

* * * *

I head for the side of the mansion, dragging my suitcase behind me. If no one's answering the front door, there's probably someone in the back.

As soon as I round the corner, I realize exactly how massive the structure is. It stretches along the cliffs in rows of dark windows across a pale stone face. The farther away I get from the gravel road, the more rocky the terrain becomes. I squint down at my feet, trying to make sure I stand on grass or rock. The mud itself is too slippery.

That's what I'm doing when I hear the roar of an engine.

I jump back as white lights blind me, moving in wild arcs across my body, across the building. It's a car. *It's a car!* And it's coming for me. I scream and back up against the wall as if it can somehow protect me from the careening vehicle.

Lights flash and flicker. The stone is freezing cold through my clothes.

And then stillness.

As suddenly as the headlights appeared, they stop moving.

I'm still pinned against the mansion like a butterfly in a frame, but at least I'm still alive. A car door slams, and then there's a large shadow looming over me.

"What the fuck are you doing? You could have been killed," says the shadow.

Somehow his voice booms over the rain, as if it's above ordinary things like the weather. I open my mouth to reply, but pinned butterflies can't speak. Everyone knows this. Shock holds my throat tight even as my heart pounds out of my chest.

"You don't belong here. This is private property."

I swallow hard. "I'm Jane Mendoza. The new nanny. Today is my first day."

There's silence from the shadow. In the stretching silence he turns into a man. A large one who seems impervious to the cold. "Jane," he says, testing my name. "Mendoza."

He says it with this northeastern accent I recognize from the Uber driver. Mend-ohhh-sah. In Texas, most people were used to Mexican last names. I'm wondering if that will be different in Maine. Maybe I would do a better job of defending myself if I weren't about to get hypothermia, if I hadn't just traveled two thousand miles for the first time in my life.

All I can hear are the words *you don't belong here.*

I've never belonged anywhere, but definitely not on this cliffside. "I work here. I'm telling the truth. You can ask inside. If we can get inside, I'm sure Mr. Rochester will tell you."

"He will."

I can't tell if it's disbelief in his tone. "Yes, he knows I'm coming. The Bassett Agency sent me. They told him I'm coming. He's probably waiting inside for me right now."

"No," he says. "I'm not."

My stomach sinks. "You're Mr. Rochester."

"Beau Rochester." He sounds grim. "I didn't get an email, but I haven't checked lately. I've been busy with… other things."

I fumble with my phone, which is incurably wet at this point. "I can show you. They sent my resume. And then the contract? Well, that's what they told me anyway—"

He's not listening. He turns around and circles back to the driver's side of the vehicle, which I can see now isn't a car, but is instead some kind of rough-terrain four-wheel thing. There are apparently no windows, only metal bars forming a crude frame. The kind of thing a rancher might use to move around his property or a good old boy might use for recreation.

I have no idea why this particular man has one, or is out using it tonight, until he turns off the lights. The engine goes quiet. He returns to me holding something small and shivering beneath his jacket. He shoves it into my freezing hands, and I fumble with my phone before pushing it into my jeans pocket.

"Here," he says. "You're good at taking care of things, right?"

There's a spark of fur covering tiny bones. It takes me a second of curling it close to my body to realize that it's a kitten. It mews, more movement than sound, its small mouth opening to show small white teeth. "Why do you have your kitten outside in the storm?"

"It's not mine. I saw it walking along the cliffs from my window when it started raining. Then it slipped and fell over the side. It took me this long to go down and search for him."

Shock roots me to the ground. "The kitten fell off a cliff?"

"Consider this your interview. You keep the small animal alive. You get the job."

I cuddle the poor kitten close, though I'm sure my body provides precious little heat. He and I are both soaked through. "He just fell off a cliff. He needs a vet, not a bedtime story."

The man. Beau. No, I can't call him by his first name. Mr. Rochester. He makes a sweeping motion with his hand toward the vehicle. "You can take the ATV anywhere on the cape. I seriously doubt you're going to find a vet open right now."

He doesn't wait to see what my answer will be. He stalks toward the house. My suitcase lolls in a particularly large puddle. Probably everything is soaked inside. He picks it up like it weighs nothing and carries it with him. I'm left following behind, as bedraggled and lost as the kitten I'm holding. It sinks its claws into me, apparently deciding I'm the safest bet in the storm.

Mr. Rochester presses numbers on a keypad, and the door swings open.

About Skye Warren

Skye Warren is the New York Times bestselling author of dangerous romance. Her books have sold over one million copies. She makes her home in Texas with her loving family, sweet dogs, and evil cat.

For more information, visit https://www.skyewarren.com.

Discover 1001 Dark Nights

COLLECTION ONE
FOREVER WICKED by Shayla Black ~ CRIMSON TWILIGHT by
Heather Graham ~ CAPTURED IN SURRENDER by Liliana Hart ~
SILENT BITE: A SCANGUARDS WEDDING by Tina Folsom ~
DUNGEON GAMES by Lexi Blake ~ AZAGOTH by Larissa Ione ~
NEED YOU NOW by Lisa Renee Jones ~ SHOW ME, BABY by
Cherise Sinclair~ ROPED IN by Lorelei James ~ TEMPTED BY
MIDNIGHT by Lara Adrian ~ THE FLAME by Christopher Rice ~
CARESS OF DARKNESS by Julie Kenner

COLLECTION TWO
WICKED WOLF by Carrie Ann Ryan ~ WHEN IRISH EYES ARE
HAUNTING by Heather Graham ~ EASY WITH YOU by Kristen
Proby ~ MASTER OF FREEDOM by Cherise Sinclair ~ CARESS OF
PLEASURE by Julie Kenner ~ ADORED by Lexi Blake ~ HADES by
Larissa Ione ~ RAVAGED by Elisabeth Naughton ~ DREAM OF YOU
by Jennifer L. Armentrout ~ STRIPPED DOWN by Lorelei James ~
RAGE/KILLIAN by Alexandra Ivy/Laura Wright ~ DRAGON KING
by Donna Grant ~ PURE WICKED by Shayla Black ~ HARD AS
STEEL by Laura Kaye ~ STROKE OF MIDNIGHT by Lara Adrian ~
ALL HALLOWS EVE by Heather Graham ~ KISS THE FLAME by
Christopher Rice~ DARING HER LOVE by Melissa Foster ~ TEASED
by Rebecca Zanetti ~ THE PROMISE OF SURRENDER by Liliana
Hart

COLLECTION THREE
HIDDEN INK by Carrie Ann Ryan ~ BLOOD ON THE BAYOU by
Heather Graham ~ SEARCHING FOR MINE by Jennifer Probst ~
DANCE OF DESIRE by Christopher Rice ~ ROUGH RHYTHM by
Tessa Bailey ~ DEVOTED by Lexi Blake ~ Z by Larissa Ione ~
FALLING UNDER YOU by Laurelin Paige ~ EASY FOR KEEPS by
Kristen Proby ~ UNCHAINED by Elisabeth Naughton ~ HARD TO
SERVE by Laura Kaye ~ DRAGON FEVER by Donna Grant ~
KAYDEN/SIMON by Alexandra Ivy/Laura Wright ~ STRUNG UP by
Lorelei James ~ MIDNIGHT UNTAMED by Lara Adrian ~ TRICKED

MACIE by Susan Stoker ~ ENCHANTED by Lexi Blake ~ TAKE THE BRIDE by Carly Phillips ~ INDULGE ME by J. Kenner ~ THE KING by Jennifer L. Armentrout ~ QUIET MAN by Kristen Ashley ~ ABANDON by Rachel Van Dyken ~ THE OPEN DOOR by Laurelin Paige ~ CLOSER by Kylie Scott ~ SOMETHING JUST LIKE THIS by Jennifer Probst ~ BLOOD NIGHT by Heather Graham ~ TWIST OF FATE by Jill Shalvis ~ MORE THAN PLEASURE YOU by Shayla Black ~ WONDER WITH ME by Kristen Proby ~ THE DARKEST ASSASSIN by Gena Showalter

COLLECTION SEVEN
THE BISHOP by Skye Warren ~ TAKEN WITH YOU by Carrie Ann Ryan ~ DRAGON LOST by Donna Grant ~ SEXY LOVE by Carly Phillips ~ PROVOKE by Rachel Van Dyken ~ RAFE by Sawyer Bennett ~ THE NAUGHTY PRINCESS by Claire Contreras ~ THE GRAVEYARD SHIFT by Darynda Jones ~ CHARMED by Lexi Blake ~ SACRIFICE OF DARKNESS by Alexandra Ivy ~ THE QUEEN by Jen Armentrout ~ BEGIN AGAIN by Jennifer Probst ~ VIXEN by Rebecca Zanetti ~ SLASH by Laurelin Paige ~ THE DEAD HEAT OF SUMMER by Heather Graham ~ WILD FIRE by Kristen Ashley ~ MORE THAN PROTECT YOU by Shayla Black ~ LOVE SONG by Kylie Scott ~ CHERISH ME by J. Kenner ~ SHINE WITH ME by Kristen Proby

COLLECTION EIGHT
DRAGON REVEALED by Donna Grant ~ CAPTURED IN INK by Carrie Ann Ryan ~ SECURING JANE by Susan Stoker ~ WILD WIND by Kristen Ashley ~ DARE TO TEASE by Carly Phillips ~ VAMPIRE by Rebecca Zanetti ~ MAFIA KING by Rachel Van Dyken ~ THE GRAVEDIGGER'S SON by Darynda Jones ~ FINALE by Skye Warren ~ MEMORIES OF YOU by J. Kenner ~ SLAYED BY DARKNESS by Alexandra Ivy ~ TREASURED by Lexi Blake ~ THE DAREDEVIL by Dylan Allen ~ BOND OF DESTINY by Larissa Ione ~ MORE THAN POSSESS YOU by Shayla Black ~ HAUNTED HOUSE by Heather Graham ~ MAN FOR ME by Laurelin Paige ~ THE RHYTHM METHOD by Kylie Scott ~ JONAH BENNETT by Tijan ~ CHANGE WITH ME by Kristen Proby ~ THE DARKEST DESTINY by Gena Showalter

On Behalf of 1001 Dark Nights,

Liz Berry, M.J. Rose, and Jillian Stein would like to thank ~

Steve Berry
Doug Scofield
Benjamin Stein
Kim Guidroz
Social Butterfly PR
Asha Hossain
Chris Graham
Chelle Olson
Kasi Alexander
Jessica Saunders
Dylan Stockton
Kate Boggs
Richard Blake
and Simon Lipskar

Made in the USA
Middletown, DE
02 August 2022